"I Love You, Leah."

His words hung in the air as Leah's heart missed a beat.

"You do?" Her voice was a whisper.

"Yes, I do. I love you from your wonderful mind to your beautiful body, all the way down to your artistic soul. I'd be very happy if you loved me back, but I don't expect it."

Leah pulled back to search his face. It was true, he did not seem to be demanding anything of her.

A deep feeling of joy welled up within her. He loved her. And she loved him. That should make everything so simple. But it wasn't simple. She could not make her declaration of love to him.

CHELSEY FORREST
is a new writer for Silhouette. She lives with her husband and two young daughters in a small town near Nashville, Tennessee.

Dear Reader:

I'd like to take this opportunity to thank you for all your support and encouragement of Silhouette Romances.

Many of you write in regularly, telling us what you like best about Silhouette, which authors are your favorites. This is a tremendous help to us as we strive to publish the best contemporary romances possible.

All the romances from Silhouette Books are for you, so enjoy this book and the many stories to come.

Karen Solem
Editor-in-Chief
Silhouette Books

CHELSEY FORREST
An Artist's Touch

Silhouette **Romance**

Published by Silhouette Books New York

America's Publisher of Contemporary Romance

SILHOUETTE BOOKS, a Division of Simon & Schuster, Inc.
1230 Avenue of the Americas, New York, N.Y. 10020

Copyright © 1984 by Chelsey Forrest

Distributed by Pocket Books

ISBN: 0-671-57272-5

First Silhouette Books printing January, 1984

10 9 8 7 6 5 4 3 2 1

Map by Ray Lundgren

SILHOUETTE, SILHOUETTE ROMANCE and colophon are
registered trademarks of Simon & Schuster, Inc.

America's Publisher of Contemporary Romance

Printed in the U.S.A.

An Artist's Touch

Chapter One

The wind whipped through the open windows of Leah DuChaine's shiny green Volvo as she motored her way south along U. S. Route 1. A dozen silver-blonde strands had worked loose from the twist at the back of her head, and they fanned out around her face in disarray. Occasionally, she lifted a hand from the steering wheel to tuck a strand of hair behind an ear. She was enjoying the feel of the warm, windy air too much to consider rolling up the windows.

Several hours earlier she had crossed the border from Georgia into Florida and had watched red clay turn into sandy loam and soil. The oaks and magnolia trees that she had seen in Georgia were still present, but the farther south she traveled, the more she saw of tall needlelike pines and Sabal palms. She had wended her way through heavy traffic in Jacksonville and was now passing through various small Floridian cities. Her heart beat faster as she mentally ticked off the last three towns before her destination. Sebastian, Wabasso, Gifford. A few more miles and she sped past the sign she was looking for: WELCOME TO VERO BEACH.

Her deep-blue eyes sparkled silver as she smiled at a sudden thought. It probably was a bit strange that she was so excited about her arrival in this quiet little Florida town in its off season. After all, she had just spent two years in the most exciting cities of Europe. Paris, Rome, Madrid. She had come into daily contact with the most inspiring architecture, the finest art and the best cuisine, even on her limited budget. She had met and talked with many interesting and worldly people. Her second year had been spent entirely in Florence, studying oil painting with an expert on glazes. Vero Beach could not compare in excitement even to Florida's larger resort cities, such as Miami or West Palm Beach.

But that was the whole point as far as Leah was concerned. She had fed voraciously for two years on the excitement of Europe, had been inspired by the works and ideas of other artists, but now she knew she needed something else. She wanted some time completely to herself, uninterrupted hours in which she could explore the creativity within herself, to see what she could produce without benefit of a lot of outside stimulation. It was just an idea that she had, an idea she thought was worth trying. And she had plenty of time to experiment with her life, for she had determined to paint with all the passion and dedication of which she was capable and to involve herself with nothing else.

She had chosen Vero Beach for her sojourn because she was not totally unfamiliar with it. Ten years before, when she was fifteen and her sister was eighteen, her family had spent a week in Vero Beach.

The vacation had been a rarity for them, for her parents could afford few such indulgences, but she remembered it as a time of peaceful happiness. This time, she had chosen the month of August because vacationing with the winter crowds of tourists would have defeated her purpose. Christmastime, when the coast was filled with tourists from the colder northern cities, was the busiest time of the year. Not as many people desired to battle the shimmering heat of August. But Leah knew she would not be too uncomfortable. It was hot, yes, at least eighty-five degrees, but that was not unbearable, and her hotel, the same hotel her family had chosen, was perched right on the edge of the cool Atlantic.

She remembered that there was a small market close to the hotel, and she pulled into its parking lot when she spotted it. She carefully got out of the car, placed her hands on the small of her back and stretched her body, which felt stiff after many hours of driving. She had driven straight from Charlotte, North Carolina, with few rest stops along the way. Her slim body was clad in black jeans and a cool white tank top. She smoothed her hair back from her face and went into the market.

She bought a box of crackers, a round of yellow cheese and a bottle of apple juice. That would be enough for that night. She had considered getting a room with a kitchenette in the new section of the hotel, as her family had done, but she really had wanted to stay in the older section. The older rooms were more interesting and picturesque and were directly on the beach, though they were without kitchenettes. She had opted for the charm of the older section and would therefore be going out for most of her food. If she decided to stay a while, she would look into renting a small refrigerator for her room.

She took the brown grocery bag out to the car, slid in behind the wheel and started off again. It was but one turn and a short drive down another street before she could see the great open iron gates of the Ocean Inn. She knew the gates had been purchased in Europe, taken from an old cathedral that had been demolished. Many of the other interesting treasures that adorned the inn had been salvaged from ship-wrecks. The building itself was so weathered and old that much of it appeared to have been built of driftwood. Together with the rustling palms that sur-rounded the building, the effect was so appealing that the newer parts of the hotel had been deliberately constructed so as to resemble the more worn and ancient sections.

Leah drove through the gates and parked close to the small wooden building that served as the recep-tion area. She entered the building and received a warm greeting from the dark-haired, dark-skinned woman at the desk.

"You must be Leah DuChaine! You're the only guest we're expecting today. I'm Joyce Becker, the owner of the Ocean Inn."

"Yes, I remember," said Leah in a friendly voice. "I was here ten years ago. It was the last time my sister and my parents and I vacationed as a family. It was wonderful."

"Let's see—" Joyce Becker turned a page in the register. "We've given you a room on the second story with a balcony overlooking the sea."

"It sounds perfect," said Leah.

"The breakfast room is on the first floor, and the back steps lead down to the patio."

"I'm sure I'll love it," said Leah. "I'm looking forward to seeing what interesting treasures the room contains. I was able to look at some of the older rooms when I was here. I especially loved all the little colorful tiles, set in unusual places, on inside walls and out—''

"People who have been here before always want to come back," said Joyce, pleased. "When my husband and I first saw the Ocean Inn twenty years ago, we fell in love with it. It was unlike any other hotel we'd seen. I wish he could see how our gamble paid off. The hotel gets more and more popular every year."

She looked up over Leah's head and said a warm hello to someone who had just come in the door. Leah did not bother to glance at the newcomer but bent over the register to sign her name.

Joyce handed Leah a silver key on a chain attached to a small piece of driftwood. "Room 2B," she said. "Just go up those outside steps on the right side of the building. You can get in the room through the door that opens on to the balcony, or you can go through the hall and enter from the door on the inside."

"I'll help her with her bags, Joyce." A deep masculine voice sounded from behind Leah. Leah turned and found herself looking up into the warm brown eyes of an exceedingly tall, strikingly handsome brown-haired man. To her surprise, Leah's heart thudded awkwardly as she fixed her eyes on his large, strongly cut features. His tan was dark and even, his wind-ruffled hair was sun lightened at the ends, and his lips curved into a self-possessed smile. He was dressed in a dark blue polo shirt and tan slacks.

"Oh, no, thank you," protested Leah. "I only have one bag. I can carry it myself."

"It's no trouble at all," said the tall man, and he opened the door and waited expectantly for Leah to precede him outside.

"Well," Leah began as she found herself ducking under the well-muscled arm that held the door open,

"I do have a few other things besides my suitcase. They're rather bulky, and I *would* appreciate your help."

Leah stepped out into the glare of the parking lot, the dark stranger close behind her. She could almost feel his eyes on her, and when she reached her car, she turned to look up at him. His eyes floated lazily over her slim form, slightly narrowed, as if he were appraising her. She cursed herself when she reached up to touch her hair, realizing that he would interpret this action as nervousness or vanity. And vain was one thing that Leah DuChaine was not.

Leah inserted her key into the trunk of the Volvo. The top swung up to reveal a stack of brilliant white canvases stretched tightly on large frames.

"An interesting cargo," commented the tall man. "You're an artist?"

Leah nodded and began lifting the canvases out one by one and stacking them neatly in his outstretched arms. She then hoisted a large burlap bag out of a corner of the trunk and swung it heavily up to shoulder height. "Art supplies," she said briefly.

"I'll take that, too." The man slung the heavy bag over one shoulder.

Leah was prepared to slam the hood shut when she noticed something in the corner of the trunk that she had not seen before. She reached in and pulled out a small cooler. She lifted off the top and found a large bottle of champagne nestled on the ice inside.

"Mother did this," she said with surprise. She looked up at the stranger and explained. "My mother was dead set against my coming down here on my own. I had just come back from two years abroad, and I think she expected me to stay with my father and her for longer than a month after that. This is a sort of peace offering, I think."

"A splendid one."

"Yes. It should be nice and fizzy after that ride!"

Leah then took her suitcase from the back seat of the car, and holding it in one hand and the cooler in the other, stared perplexed at the grocery bag, which was still in the front seat. She looked up to see that the stranger had two fingers extended as he retained his hold on the canvases and art supplies.

"If you'll just hook that cooler over these two fingers," he suggested, "I think we'll be able to make it."

Leah suppressed a giggle as she complied with his request. She was half tempted to pile her suitcase and the grocery bag into his arms, too, just to see if he would complain. Something told her he would not. She headed toward the stairs that led to her room, followed by her benefactor.

"Interesting place, isn't it?" said the man conversationally.

"I just love it," returned Leah. Deep, gentle noises came from the old iron bells they brushed past as they made their way up the weather-beaten wooden steps. "Are you staying here, too?"

"Oh, no. I'm a friend of Joyce Becker. Just stopped in to say hello to her."

Leah opened her mouth to ask further questions of the stranger, then stopped herself. She was glad for the help the man was giving her, but she knew she didn't want to get further involved than that. Her whole purpose in coming here had been to escape distractions.

They came to the top of the stairs, to the deck, which stretched the entire length of the back of the hotel. Directly below was a narrow strip of beach with a few sunbathers, and beyond was the gray and green vastness of the Atlantic. A warm, steady wind blew in from the water. Leah longed to stop and stand with arms outstretched to embrace the wind, but she busied herself with trying to fit the silver key into the door of room 2B.

"Here, I'll do that." The handsome stranger set the canvases down, and with two strides he was at Leah's side. He shook the door and jiggled the key in the lock till finally the door swung inward. "There we go."

Leah entered the room and switched on the lights while the stranger gathered up the canvases and carried them in behind her. For a moment, his large frame was silhouetted in the doorway, and Leah felt an inexplicable flash of panic. There was something about the sight of his looming figure, about to enter the small room, that made her wonder if she should have accepted his help. She knew it was silly to think he would try to hurt her in this place, but he was a stranger, after all, and one of greater than average size and strength.

Or was it something other than his powerful build that frightened her? She noticed that her pulse sped up alarmingly when she looked into his dark, amused eyes.

A low whistle from her companion brought her back to reality. He had put the canvases carefully on the floor and was gazing about the room with interest. "It certainly is unique, isn't it!"

The large double bed, of polished walnut, was the only traditional piece of furniture in the room. The dresser was tall and narrow, with a double row of drawers whose pulls were blue porcelain. Next to the dresser was an irregularly shaped bench that looked as if it had been made of a large slab of driftwood that someone had sanded and set on legs. The walls were covered in a wallpaper subtly striped in grays and blues, and arrayed on them were various maritime objects and objets d'art. Over the bed hung the focal point of the room, a large, beautifully rendered picture of a foreign port, probably European. A pleased smile touched Leah's lips as she realized that the seemingly haphazard collection of furniture and objects in the room *worked,* in an aesthetically interesting way.

"Yes, it's very nicely done," she answered her companion. "Well!" She turned in a businesslike manner and extended her hand. "I thank you very much, Mr.—"

"Cambridge, Taylor Cambridge," returned the man, shaking her hand gravely. He watched her as if to gauge her reaction. When there was no sign of recognition from her, he seemed obscurely pleased. "Please call me Taylor. And you are—?"

"Leah DuChaine."

"DuChaine," repeated Taylor, giving the name a perfect French pronunciation. "There's a DuChaine in Marseilles. A count, I believe."

Leah burst into laughter. "My father's a bricklayer in Charlotte, North Carolina," she said. "Now, if you'll excuse me—"

"Dismissing me?" asked Taylor in a soft voice.

Leah gave an irritated shrug. "I see no reason for you to stay," she said. "I'm sure I can manage my unpacking by myself." She tried to keep her eyes lowered, off his face, for there was something compelling about his gaze. Finally, she looked up at him, at his dark eyes fringed with black lashes and the smile playing across his mouth. She realized that behind his controlled façade he was laughing at her.

"As you wish," he said easily. "But tell me—how long do you plan to stay? Perhaps we can arrange to meet again."

"Oh, I don't think so," Leah said, but she knew her

tone was unconvincing. She put more authority into her voice. "I really came here to get away, to be able to spend some time by myself. It's nothing personal, you understand."

"What a coincidence." Taylor chuckled. "I come to Vero Beach myself for that very reason, to escape. But perhaps we can spend some of our time alone—together." He lifted his eyebrows mischievously.

Leah felt anger rising slowly inside of her. This tall, good-looking, magnetic man was spoiling everything! All she wanted was to be left alone, and she hadn't been here fifteen minutes before he had intruded.

But that wasn't really what was making her angry. She was used to fending off unwelcome advances with aplomb. Her blonde, blue-eyed beauty had always attracted men, and she had always known how to handle them. Why, then, was this man making it so difficult for her? She hated to admit it, but there was something dangerously attractive about him, his unsettling good looks, his offhand but masterful manner, his powerful maleness. She was angry at herself for handling the situation so poorly, for sending out unspoken signals that said she was interested, when what she really wanted to say was "no."

"I prefer to spend my time truly alone," said Leah in a low voice.

"I understand completely," came back Taylor. "But surely you have nothing so pressing planned for this evening that you can't sacrifice one or two hours to having dinner with me."

What a nerve you have, thought Leah. *You don't seem to understand when a woman is saying no*. But she knew to her chagrin that her wide blue eyes were saying maybe. And there was the bottle of champagne sitting where she had placed it on the dresser, seeming to issue a bold, silent hint. Finally, she said, "I really had planned to have a light snack alone here tonight. But I suppose it won't hurt anything for me to offer you a glass of champagne."

"I'd love to," replied Taylor with exaggerated politeness, as if to mock her ungracious offer. "I'll go wangle a couple of champagne glasses out of the headwaiter. Joyce won't mind a bit." He eyed the grocery bag, which was on the dresser next to the champagne. "Do we need plates, too?"

"One plate," said Leah with a sigh. "And a knife."

"I'll be right back."

Leah telephoned her mother in Charlotte to notify her of her safe arrival—and to thank her for the champagne. Her mother told her that several people had called and asked for her.

"You didn't tell anyone where I am, did you?"

"No." Her mother sighed. "Janie called, and a young man who didn't leave his name. They couldn't understand why your own mother doesn't know where you are."

"I'm sorry, mom. It won't last forever. I just need to be alone for a while, with no phone calls, no distractions. I appreciate your helping me out on this."

Leah's father insisted on speaking to her, too. She knew her parents missed her and found it hard to accept the fact that she had been on her own for several years.

After she hung up the phone, she quickly unpacked her suitcase. She placed her clothes in the dresser drawers and hung the three dressier outfits she had brought with her in the closet. She had not brought much with her, just a set of very casual clothes and two dresses and a skirt-and-blouse set, which were a concession to her occasional desire to dine in a nice restaurant. Most of her clothes were in neutral colors or in black or white. Leah had taken to wearing such noncolors not because she disliked color but because she was not interested in drawing attention to herself. She wished nothing more than to be an artist's hands, an artist's eye, an artist's brain. She loved to see a daring use of color in the clothing that other women wore, but she just didn't want to fuss over herself. It was for this reason that she wore her hair pulled back tightly from her face and used very little makeup.

In some corner of her mind, she was vaguely aware that she presented a striking figure in spite of her lack of effort. Her black clothing provided an arresting contrast to her pale blondeness, and the severe hair style revealed the perfect structure and lovely creamy skin of her face. Her dark blue eyes and thick lashes needed little makeup to enhance them.

Taylor returned in a few minutes and stood in the doorway holding the glasses and plate. "Why don't we eat out here on the balcony?" he suggested. "There are two rocking chairs and a table."

Leah nodded in agreement. She piled the cheese and crackers on the plate and brought it out to the tiny table. Taylor set the champagne and glasses on the table, and the two of them took their seats. Leah sat rather tensely, but Taylor seemed as relaxed as if he had known her for years.

"Watch out," he cautioned, holding the champagne bottle away from his body and pointing it over the deck railing. The cork flew off with a resounding pop and surprisingly little spillage.

Taylor poured the pale heady liquid into each glass. Then he leaned forward, one eyebrow cocked in amusement. "Now tell me," he demanded, "just what is it we're celebrating?"

"A new beginning for me," she said lightly. "A

decision to truly dedicate my life to what I want to achieve."

"An impressive aim," he murmured. "Let's drink to it."

They sat quietly for a few minutes, sipping the champagne from the Ocean Inn's delicate shallow glasses. Leah looked out to sea, vaguely aware that her companion's eyes were focused on her.

After a few swallows of champagne, she began to relax. "I don't have it very often, but champagne is my favorite drink," she confessed.

"I'm not surprised," he returned, smiling. The knife glinted as he held it poised in midair. "May I slice you some of this excellent *fromage,* madame?"

"Please, kind sir," she replied, entering into the game. "And place it on one of those exquisitely baked crackers!"

Taylor picked up one of the standard grocery-store-type crackers and studied it with a quizzical look. Leah laughed, arching her back against the rocking chair and giving it a few slight rocks. She watched her companion as he prepared her cracker and offered it to her, going through all the motions with a courtly air. She smiled, having decided that she might as well enjoy this interlude with Taylor, since it had proved to be inevitable.

The cheese and crackers really were good, and they ate them with pleasure. The warm winds blew in from the rhythmic sea and caressed their faces delightfully. The sky began to darken, and the tips of the ocean waves turned pink as they captured some color from the sunset that was now taking place on the other side of the building.

"It's too bad we can't see the sunset on this side," he remarked.

"Oh, not at all!" she disagreed. "This is just perfect."

"Do you really mean that?" He shot her an inquiring glance.

"Oh, yes! There's no place else I'd rather be right now."

She had meant that remark in all sincerity, but she wished she could take it back as she suddenly realized how he might interpret it. Surely he would understand that she was referring to the sounds and smells of the beach, the dark beauty of the sea! He could not be so arrogant as to think his presence was an important ingredient in her enjoyment of her surroundings. That was not what she had meant at all.

She stole a look at the man who sat beside her in the shadows as he gazed out to sea. His profile was strong and commanding, as was the rest of him—his nose somewhat prominent, his chin firm, his brow rugged. He turned his head, caught her looking at him and gave her a gentle smile.

Gentle? From this intrusive, demanding person? But so it was, and she felt herself actually warming to him a bit.

"What are you thinking, Blue Eyes?"

She merely shook her head.

"Well, then, tell me some more about what you plan to do with yourself. I'm interested in this great—dedication of yours." The trace of amusement was back in his voice.

"I'm just determined," she said slowly, "to be an artist. A painter. And nothing is going to stand in my way."

"That's admirable," he said matter-of-factly. "But you make it sound as if people are conspiring to throw obstacles in your path from all directions."

"It's not as easy as you think," she insisted. She took a deep breath. She was on the verge of telling him about her talented older sister Eve, who had lost her ambition and traded a promising career as a water-colorist for a comfortable marriage. In Leah's opinion, Eve had lost on that transaction, and she herself was determined that she would not give up her ambitions for any reason whatsoever. But somehow she felt sure that the confident man seated beside her would not understand, and she did not wish to be the object of his amusement. So she said stiffly, "I just don't want to jeopardize my career by getting too involved with anything else. I don't want to break my concentration."

Taylor chuckled softly. "Does this fine dedication exclude romantic entanglements, also?" he inquired.

Leah floundered a moment, then said, "Yes." This was a subject that she had not worked out to her own satisfaction. She knew that marriage and children would definitely hinder her career, but there were times, usually at night, when she did have certain vague longings. For some of her friends, casual sex was the answer, but Leah couldn't accept that for herself. Besides, she knew that her longings were more far-reaching than that, and she wasn't quite sure what it would take to satisfy them—or to cast them out.

"That's a shame," said Taylor, smiling. Once again, his bold brown eyes roamed over her figure till she felt distinctly uncomfortable—and the warm feeling within her had begun to spread. Was it due to the champagne or his warm gaze?

"Now tell me about yourself," urged Leah, picking up the last cracker and starting to nibble on it.

Taylor shrugged as if to dismiss the importance of

the subject. "I live in the East," he said. "I get tired of the crush of people occasionally—and I spend a little time here."

"Do you have a place in Vero Beach?" she asked.

"Yes, I have a place."

"One of the condominiums?" When Leah had arrived earlier that day, she had been able to make out the tops of some modern condominiums that jutted into the sky some distance down the beach. Even now, in the dark, it would be possible to see their lights shining if one were on the beach.

"No, it's not a condominium," he answered.

Leah concluded silently that Taylor must own one of the little cottages that lined the beach in places.

"I'm interested in these principles of yours," said Taylor. "Do they dictate that you dine alone, or might you have dinner with a friend?"

"Of course I eat with friends!" said Leah testily. Just as she had feared, he was turning the whole thing into a joke.

"Not just female friends?" he pressed.

She shook her head wearily.

"Then would you accept an invitation to dine with me tomorrow night? I feel we've become friends this evening, don't you? And such a delightful evening it's been . . ."

"No, no, no!" burst out Leah angrily. "I may not be a hermit, but I told you I plan to spend my time alone." She rose to her feet. At the same time, Taylor rose to his. He towered over her.

"You don't want to see me again, then," he said.

"No."

Taylor stared at her for a long moment. "Then why do I get the feeling—" He spoke slowly and moved just a fraction closer to Leah as her heart began to hammer. "Why do I get the very strong feeling that you want me to kiss you?"

Leah looked at him, blue eyes wide with amazement. He took a step closer, took her chin in his hand and tilted her face up to his. His mouth came down sweetly and strongly on her soft lips, and with his kiss he began to extinguish the resistance inside her. His mouth was hot and searching; his powerful arms enfolded her and drew her in close so that her body was pressed tightly to his and she was almost on tiptoe. He parted her lips with his tongue and explored the sweetness of her mouth. The warmth within her that had begun earlier in the evening grew to a dangerous heat that enveloped her entire body. She was keenly aware of strong hands stroking her back, of her breasts pressed against his chest, of the breathtaking kiss that made her forget everything else. Her senses were saturated with the thrilling nearness of this man, of his male scent and warmth. Then he pulled back abruptly, his eyes intent on her face.

"All right, Miss Blue Eyes," he said in a voice like rough velvet. "If you don't want to see me again, just say so."

Leah opened her mouth but could not speak.

"I'll be here tomorrow night," he said good-naturedly. "At seven."

Then he turned and left. Leah could hear his footfalls as he went down the stairs at the side of the building and out into the parking lot. She heard the roar of an engine coming to life; then the car was gone.

Numbly, she gathered up the dishes on the table to take them inside. She could hear the low voices of people sitting on the patio directly below the deck. It seemed strange to her that for a moment she had completely forgotten the outside world, but people were talking, wind chimes were tinkling, the ocean was whispering, and the stars shone in the dark blue sky. She turned on the lights as she entered her room, then sat on the bed, chin on her fist, very preoccupied. What had happened to her? she wondered. She vowed to herself that she would not go out with Taylor the following night. He simply presumed too much. He had taken her by surprise with his sudden kiss, but she would be on her guard from then on. He was much too arrogant for her taste.

She wandered into the bathroom and turned on a hot shower. She removed her clothes, then stepped into the shower, allowing the steaming water to cascade over her body and run down its curves in small streams. She lathered herself slowly, the heat and the steam soothing her troubled nerves.

Once out of the shower, she rubbed herself dreamily with a large white towel. Then she removed the pins from her hair one by one, and her hair fell loosely about her shoulders. She reached for the gauzy nightshirt in which she slept, but before she grasped it, something made her turn to look in the large mirror over the sinks. She stopped and stared at her reflection, mesmerized.

The steam from her shower had fogged up the perimeter of the mirror, so she looked as if she had just emerged from a cloud of mist. Her silver-blonde hair made a shimmering halo about her face. She stared into her own silver-flecked, deep blue eyes, then looked at the rest of her body, rosy and shining from her shower. Her eyes wandered over her graceful curves and rested on her rose-tinted breasts and smooth thighs. An inexplicable feeling of sadness came over her as she became, for perhaps the first time, fully aware of the beauty she possessed. Dangerously, she began to contemplate the possibility of allowing someone to enjoy her beauty intimately, and she wondered if she was wrong in her determination never to allow another to possess her in that way. She began to wonder what it would be like . . .

But at what cost? a voice within her cried. She pulled her thin nightshirt off the hook on the door and slipped into it.

She walked out into the room and over to the stack of canvases. After she arranged them about the room, resting them against the walls, she leaned back on her bed and surveyed the smooth white surfaces with contentment. There was potential there—before she ever applied a paint-charged brush to the linen surfaces—and she enjoyed thinking of the colors and forms that she would bring to life.

She had intended to do much of her work at night—but not that night. It was a night for anticipation, for savoring the idea of freedom, of unrestricted creativity.

She slid between the sheets on the large comfortable bed, switched out the lamp on the bedside table and began to drift off to sleep. As she reached that tentative stage between wakefulness and slumber, an image of Taylor Cambridge rudely entered her thoughts, as the man himself had done in reality that evening. She turned uneasily in her bed and gave a sigh. Finally, she slept.

Chapter Two

The next day found Leah on the shallow beach in back of the hotel, hard at work under a brightly striped canvas umbrella. She wore a black maillot with a loose white shirt as a cover-up. She sat cross-legged on a beach blanket, peering through a pair of large sunglasses that overpowered the delicate structure of her face. She held a pad of newsprint in her lap, propped against her knees, and skillfully slashed and smudged its surface with a piece of soft charcoal, capturing on paper the natural forms, human and otherwise, that she saw about her. She carefully delineated the dark shadows in her sketches, leaving much of the paper white to indicate the bleaching effect of the hot sun.

A flash of color caught her eye, and she noticed a golden-tanned girl in a deep lavender bikini racing across the beach to the water's edge. She smiled at the pleasing colors of the girl, the lavender and the gold.

The girl's figure was shapely, and she took an appealingly awkward pose at the edge of the sand, looking out to sea. Leah turned to a fresh piece of newsprint and worked rapidly to capture the pose on paper.

As Leah was finishing up the sketch, she sensed that someone had come up behind her and was looking over her shoulder as she drew. She kept her head bent over her work. She was used to having people wander up to see her work when she sketched in public, and the presence of onlookers in no way hindered her or made her nervous. She paused for a moment to view what she had done, her piece of charcoal held lightly in her slim fingers, poised above the paper, ready to descend back to its surface if she should see that the drawing required further work. It was then that the person behind her spoke, in a deep masculine voice, faintly amused but admiring.

"You're very good."

Leah glanced up to see Taylor Cambridge, clad in a pair of brief black swim trunks, standing behind her. His tanned muscular body gleamed in the hot sun; his dark eyes were half closed against the glare; his arms were folded across his chest. Leah instinctively moved her hand to cover her work, then pulled it back, determined not to appear flustered by his sudden appearance. With Taylor's gaze on the work she had just completed, she suddenly became aware of the sensual appeal of the sketch of the meagerly clad girl; up till then, her concern had been an aesthetic one, focusing on a graceful form in an interesting pose. She wondered if Taylor could even understand her artistic intent or if his compliment was due entirely to male admiration of a scantily dressed female.

"Thank you."

"May I?" Taylor lowered himself to the ground and sat casually on the blanket beside Leah.

"I have little choice, I see," said Leah dryly.

Taylor grinned at her and brushed her cheek lightly with the back of his hand. "Come on, Miss Artistic Genius, you know better than that. A little fraternization with the opposite sex never ended any artist's career. I won't stay long, though. I'll let you get some work done so you'll feel better about your dinner date with me tonight."

"I'm sorry, I can't have dinner with you tonight," Leah said firmly.

"But you agreed to——"

"Agreed to!" she exclaimed. "You tricked me into it!"

"Tricked you?" he repeated, both eyebrows raised high. "And how did I accomplish that?"

Leah compressed her lips. She couldn't very well say, "You turned me into jelly with your kiss so that I didn't have the strength to say no!"

"I mean to stand by my original plans," she said with conviction, "and those plans do *not* include you."

The minute the words were out of her mouth, she wished she could snatch them back. She meant every word she said, but she wished her phrasing had not been quite so abrupt.

But Taylor just gave a low chuckle. Again, she felt his touch as he teased the skin just below her neck with his finger tips. "Have dinner with me," he coaxed. "You won't regret it."

"I have no intention——" she began, but she was interrupted by the arrival of a third person. It was the girl in the lavender bikini. She approached them eagerly.

"Michael!" squealed the girl.

Leah stared hard at her. It must be a matter of mistaken identity. But the girl had taken hold of

Taylor's arm and was laughingly pulling him to his feet. And she was calling him by a new name.

"Michael, you came back to see me!" she was saying with delight. She threw a brief glance in Leah's direction, then continued to ignore her as she tried to maneuver Taylor away from the blanket. Leah waited patiently for Taylor to correct the girl's mistake. But no, he was laughing, too. He actually knew her.

"Sherry, I didn't see you at first! No, I can't come with you now." He looked down at Leah and tried to catch her eye. But Leah's face was set like stone, and she kept her eyes on the newsprint before her.

"Well, maybe I *can* come with you right now," said Taylor softly, and allowing the girl to hold on to one of his arms, he set off with her. Raising her eyes surreptitiously, Leah watched the two lean, tanned bodies moving down the beach.

Well, that takes care of that, she thought with relief after she lost sight of them. Her lip curled with disdain. That giddy girl was probably just the kind of girl that Taylor—or Michael—was looking for. How strange it was that he had lied about his name. She saw no good reason for it, but at least he was gone.

Leah flipped the page of newsprint over to the back of the pad and began to work on another drawing.

Only three-quarters of an hour passed before Taylor came striding back down the beach—alone. Leah glanced up, her look of disbelief hidden by the cumbersome sunglasses as Taylor walked toward her. Once again, he stood towering over her, his eyes riveted to her face. Leah's heart gave a little lurch as she waited for him to speak.

There was a half smile on Taylor's lips. "I'm sorry for running off like that, Leah," he began. "I lost my temper for a moment—you just won't thaw, will you?"

Leah closed her pad of newsprint and set it down beside her. "You don't owe me anything," she said. "An explanation or an apology or—anything."

"And you don't owe me anything, right?" he asked. "Isn't that what you're about to say next? Well, I agree with you. But Leah"—his voice grew deep and persuasive—"I'm not asking for so much. Just the pleasure of your company. You can't deny that there's something there between us. You must have felt it last night. Why don't we explore that attraction, at least for one evening? If we find there's nothing really there, we never have to see each other again."

Something was smoldering inside of Leah's still body. She felt very strongly that Taylor was asking for more, much more, than just the "pleasure of her company" for one evening. She fought the contradicting emotions within herself. In spite of her intended aloofness, when she examined her feelings honestly, she knew there was something inside her that responded to this forthright man, some stirring within her that his words and, the previous night, his touch had set aflame. For several moments, she was mute, sifting a handful of sand through her fingers. Then:

"Who are you—Taylor or Michael?" she burst out.

Taylor laughed. Seeing some encouragement in her abrupt question, he dropped to the ground beside her. He lowered his voice and spoke close to her ear.

"My real name is Taylor Cambridge," he said. "Sherry—and a few others—know me as Michael Slayton."

"I suppose there's a perfectly understandable reason for that," she said coolly.

"As it happens, there is." He smiled. "Sometimes, when people know who I am, they begin to want more from me than I'm willing to give. Sometimes I want to relax and enjoy myself with a person, without any pressures or promises . . ."

Leah shrugged. "Who are you?" she asked in an innocent tone.

Taylor threw back his head and laughed.

"*I've* certainly never heard of you," Leah went on.

"And there's no reason why you should have," he said, "unless you're an avid reader of gossip columns. Some of the columnists take great pleasure in zeroing in on almost every move I make—who I'm seen with, imagined matrimonial plans, financial dealings. You'd think that the movie stars and politicians would provide enough grist for their mill and that they'd leave me alone. They seem to forget that I'm a simple businessman."

Leah restrained an impulse to laugh at Taylor's humble evaluation of himself. It was evident that Taylor traveled in high circles, that he was wealthy and had achieved a measure of fame—or notoriety. But she was really not interested in learning any more about him. Despite her initial attraction to him, she knew she could never trust a man who used a false name to get what he wanted. And what this man wanted, she was sure, was pleasure—with no strings attached.

"Perhaps you can tell me, then," she ventured, "why you told me your real name—and I assume it is your real name. Why did you decide not to use your . . . alias . . . with me?"

"I'm not sure," he replied. "It could be that I knew you were the kind of woman I would never want to lie to."

"Oh, very smooth," she remarked. "I commend you."

"Nonetheless, I am sincere," he said, his gaze

dark-eyed and steady. "And I really would like to know you better. My relationships with the people who know me as Michael Slayton seem to remain rather superficial."

Leah tightened her lips knowingly, but Taylor seemed not to notice.

"You don't mind if I sit here with you while you draw, do you?" he asked.

Leah shrugged her assent. She turned to her pad again; then a notion struck her. "I'll draw you," she said. "Here. Sit just like that and turn your head that way. Look at the ocean."

"I'm not sure how long I can hold still," said Taylor, but he complied with her request.

"This won't take long at all."

Leah attacked the blank sheet of paper with vigor, a half-formed, somewhat cruel idea in the back of her mind. She remembered sketching a young fellow once many years before, a boy of whom she was not particularly fond. Somehow it all came out in the drawing, not deliberately, but the result had been a most unflattering portrait and enough of a likeness to crush thoroughly the poor young fellow. Perhaps she could accomplish the same sort of thing with the arrogant Taylor Cambridge. No one was so handsome that his looks could not be distorted slightly for the worse. She did not pause to wonder why she felt the need to hurt Taylor, or at least to take him down a peg or two. She felt a kind of power when she exercised her talent, though it was not her custom to use it to hurt people.

To her dismay, the likeness that emerged beneath her moving charcoal was boldly attractive. She had begun by slashing in the lines of Taylor's confident profile, had intended to exaggerate a line here and there. But she ended by carefully stroking in the masculine planes and angles of his face, the shadows of his eyes, the square jaw, the strong neck, the powerful shape of his naked shoulders.

"There, it's done," said Leah flatly. She handed the drawing to Taylor, and he studied it for a minute, a faint smile on his lips, but he had little to say about it.

"You *are* good" was all he said. He eased himself back on the blanket beside her till he was supporting himself on his elbows, the position throwing his shoulder muscles into relief. One leg was bent, the other long leg stretched out straight before him. At first, he appeared simply to be enjoying the soothing pleasures of the beach environment, the sea sounds and the wind ruffling his hair. Leah wondered how he could appear to be so totally relaxed, and she concluded that he must have almost forgotten her presence. Hesitantly, she began another drawing. Then he turned his head slowly to look at her, and she realized that he had been lost in thought.

"I think I understand your love for fine art," he said in a quiet voice that held none of his usual taunting manner. "The kind of creative gift that you have should be used. And if it means so much to you . . . well, you should never give it up."

A soft, unexpected glow flashed through Leah as she listened to his words. *It's hard for me to dislike him,* she thought, amused at her own reaction, *when he says a thing like that.* She was very aware of the kind interest in his eyes. She wondered if she could believe this side of him or if it, too, was a deception.

They talked a few minutes more. Taylor was courteous and attentive. He seemed to realize that Leah was looking on him with a little more favor.

"How about a short walk?" he suggested at last. "You must be tired after sitting for so long."

A short walk—just like you and golden girl, thought

Leah with contempt. But at that moment, Taylor grabbed both of her hands in his own and pulled her to her feet. The shock of his warm, strong grasp and the sudden vigor of his action made Leah laugh. "All right, you win," she said.

He retained possession of one of her hands as they set off down the beach. Leah kept on her straw hat, as it was early afternoon and the sun would be merciless on her fair skin. The sand was hot and pleasant on the soles of her feet; the sounds of the sea and the gulls spoke of wildness and freedom. Taylor pulled her into the water, and it felt cool about their ankles as they splashed through it.

She glanced up at her companion and saw Taylor looking down at her from his towering height, a glad smile creasing his tanned face, little laugh lines radiating from the corners of his smiling dark eyes. He was a devastatingly attractive man—there was no question of that. She began to enjoy the feel of his hand enfolding hers in a way that was almost protective.

Not that Leah DuChaine needed protection. More than once she had protected *herself* from the advances of a man who had begun by claiming that his primary interest was to protect her. Of course, Taylor had made no such claim, but he was definitely pursuing her—and to what end Leah thought she knew only too well. There was a chance that he was lying about his importance in the world of business, that it was just a line to attract impressionable young girls. On the other hand, it was also possible that every word he said was true, that he really did escape his high-powered world to Vero Beach occasionally for the purpose of relaxing incognito. Of course, part of his relaxation seemed to involve . . . yes, young and impressionable girls. Leah's lips curved into a proud smile, for although she was only twenty-five, she knew that she was a woman of substance. If Taylor Cambridge didn't know that by now, he would find out soon enough.

They had come so far by now that the hotels lining the beach had given way to small houses and cottages; finally, those, too, grew more sparse. They passed an elderly couple, also holding hands, walking in the opposite direction, and when they walked farther along, they saw a solitary young girl bathing a fair distance out to sea.

"Here's the point," remarked Taylor. The trees grew more thickly and closer to the sea, and the land curved outward and came to a point in the water. "This means we've come two miles."

"Good heavens! You must have been pulling me along, then! I'm not tired a bit."

"That's good." Taylor's eyes flicked her lazily. "Hey." He took her by the shoulders and turned her so that she faced him directly. "Tell me why you're so determined not to be with me."

"I thought I explained all that," she said. "It's nothing personal. I just came here to be alone. I haven't had enough time like that in my life. Please, can't you understand—I need time and concentration in order to work!"

"Come on, let's talk about it." He put his arm across her shoulders and guided her to a flat rock half secluded by some feathery palms. He pushed her gently down in front of it so that she was seated on the sand, leaning against the rock, and he sat down beside her. "Now look at this," commanded Taylor in his deep voice, stretching a long arm out to indicate the expanse of empty sea before them, its ever-changing surface and the brilliance of the sky. "Don't you need times like this just to look and contemplate? Don't you need inspiration like this in order to work?"

Leah just looked at him. This time, the amused smile was on *her* face. "I thank you very much, kind sir," she said dryly, "for being so thoughtful as to provide all this ready-made inspiration for me. I'm sure I would not have found it on my own. We artists are always looking for astute businessmen to guide us in our search for—"

"All right, all right," Taylor said, laughing. "Consider me put in my place." He leaned back, his arms crossed behind his head, setting a fascinating ripple of muscles into play. "You're really different, you know," he said, "from my idea of what an artist is like. I know the profession requires dedication, but I guess I always thought artists were more free in—that they always found time for—that their life-style was—"

"What you're trying to tell me," broke in Leah, "is that you were sure I would be an easy mark."

Taylor sat up suddenly, his eyebrows raised in amusement. "I meant no such thing," he said indignantly. "I'm sure you're a lady of highly refined scruples. You've made that very clear. There's just one thing I wish you'd do for me."

"And that is—?"

"Take those clumsy things off!" He reached quickly for her oversized sunglasses and ripped them off the bridge of her nose, then placed them at arm's length behind him on the sand. Leah gave a small shriek and lunged to retrieve them, but Taylor's hands clamped down on her shoulders, and try as she would, she could not pull free. She placed her hands on his chest to give him a mighty shove, but by now she was laughing. They were both laughing, and her struggles had become a game.

"Let me go!" she shouted; then she grew quiet as

she felt the impact of Taylor's brown eyes staring intensely into her own.

"Such blue, blue eyes," he murmured. "That's what I wanted to see."

He gazed into her eyes for the longest moment in the world, and Leah's heart began to thud dangerously. His hands relaxed their grip on her shoulders, but she remained quiet and still.

Then he leaned in close and kissed her roughly, his firm male lips forcing open her own softer ones. Leah's head fell back, and her straw hat dropped quietly to the sand behind her. Taylor groaned softly as he explored the sweetness of her mouth with his tongue and moved his hands across her shoulder blades and down the length of her back. His lips were warm and alive, his fingers alternately firm and feather light. A rough place on the rock against which Leah leaned began to press uncomfortably into her back as her body sank backward under Taylor's relentless advance. She shifted into a more comfortable, half-reclining position, and Taylor's hand moved to cradle the nape of her neck. He broke their kiss and pressed her face into the warm hollow of his neck, his lips close to her ear as he whispered, "You're so sweet."

Leah gave a ragged sigh as she entwined her arms tightly around Taylor's neck. A wave of aching desire spread through her body. Never before had she been so tempted to give in to such a powerful feeling.

Mindlessly, she tilted her head back again to receive his drugging kiss; then she kissed him back, her small tongue darting between his lips, evoking an even more passionate response from him as he covered her with hot kisses.

He slipped the soft cotton material of her shirt off her shoulder, first one, then the other, and the shirt slid down her torso and came to rest, softly crumpled about her hips. Taylor drew back a space, his eyes sparkling in appreciation of the sight that greeted him—her upper body covered only by the black maillot, which fit like a second skin. With a sigh, he rested his hands on her slender waist, then raised one and gently placed it on her chest, barely stroking, dipping just low enough to tease the hollow between her breasts at the top of her suit. She held her breath at the pleasurable sensation.

Then Taylor hooked his thumbs beneath the thin black straps that held up Leah's maillot and began to slide them off her shoulders. As his hands glided down her shoulders, a devastating thought intruded into Leah's mind.

How long had it been since Taylor had been doing exactly what he was doing now?

A little over an hour?

With the golden beauty who called him Michael?

Leah jerked violently to one side, pulling herself out of Taylor's grasp. Hurriedly, she pulled up the straps of her suit and thrust her arms back into the sleeves of her cover-up.

"What's wrong!" he demanded urgently.

"I don't know," she said angrily. "But there must be something wrong to make me let you do what you were doing now!" She scrambled to her feet.

"What *I* was doing!" he repeated, his eyes cold and furious as he stood up to his full height. "Don't start pretending that you weren't even there! You were enjoying that just as much as I was. What's the matter with you!"

"All right, I enjoyed it," she muttered. "But maybe you enjoy it a little too much—or too often—with too many people." She bent to pick up her sunglasses and hat.

Taylor stared at her blonde head as if he thought she had taken leave of her senses. "Kindly explain to me what you're talking about," he snapped. His dark eyebrows came down threateningly.

He took her by the shoulders, but she pulled free and began to run along the beach, back toward the hotel, knowing full well that Taylor could overtake her with just a few powerful strides and—and make her do anything. She glanced back over her shoulder to see him standing stock-still in the very same spot, casually watching her race down the beach. Feeling foolish, she slowed her pace and began to walk with dignity back to the hotel.

Taylor walked behind her at an unhurried pace and soon overtook her through the easy length of his strides. He fell into step beside her.

"Now explain," he said shortly.

"It's just that I refuse to be a part of your string of conquests," said Leah scathingly, "especially when it's all accomplished in the space of one afternoon! I'll bet it hasn't even been an hour since you were making love to that silly girl in the sand dunes—and now you're trying the very same thing with me! I think that's disgusting."

"That's ludicrous," he said in a voice of quiet reasonableness. "I didn't touch Sherry. I really didn't want to go off with her; you know that. But you acted as though you didn't want me around; you refused even to look at me. How could I tell her I wanted to stay with you when you were acting like that?" He gave a short laugh. "So you think I took her off in order to accomplish my evil design, dumped her on a sand dune, then ran back to seduce you, too, in my own disgusting fashion?"

"Why were you gone so long? And why did you

come back so soon?" Leah asked, realizing as she spoke the absurdity of the two conflicting questions.

"It took me that long to get rid of her," he said patiently.

"And how did you do that?"

"Simple. Her boy friend showed up."

"How convenient."

Taylor gave her a sunny smile, the warmth having returned to his brown eyes. It was as if he had never lost his temper. "You're hard to figure out," he said at last. "You give me the ice-maiden line, the virgin who will sacrifice herself to the great god Art—then, back there"—he indicated the point behind them with a jerk of his head—"you show me the passion within you that I'll bet you never even knew you had—"

"Please don't," she said softly, embarrassed.

"Believe it or not," he continued, "I'd honestly like to give you what you want—"

"I don't want to hear any more of that kind of talk," she warned.

"That's not what I mean," he said. "I mean I'd like to give you what you *really* want."

"And I suppose you're about to tell me what I really want," she said with a resigned air.

"I don't have to," he replied, "you've already told me yourself. You don't want me to talk to you, to look at you, to touch you. *This*, my dear Miss Artistic Genius, is what you want."

He folded his arms across his chest, turned his shoulders away as if to exclude Leah and took on a ferocious scowl. He strode along in silence while Leah glanced up at him with faint curiosity.

"Now isn't this nice?" growled Taylor, barely moving his lips. "I never thought noncommunication could be so much fun. I know I'm having the time of my life." He lapsed into deliberate silence again, his features darkened by his frown, refusing to look at or speak to Leah. Leah felt a spontaneous laugh welling up inside of her, and she tried to smother it with one hand.

"No, no," he warned, holding up a hand. "Laughing is not permitted. It takes up too much time, and it *ruins one's concentration.*"

Leah choked back the giggles. Then she heaved a deep sigh. "I guess I appear quite silly to you," she said.

"Oh, no, not at all," he insisted kindly. They were now a short distance from the hotel, behind which relaxed a sparse crowd of vacationers. He stopped her with a light touch on her arm and turned her to him. He looked directly into her eyes as he spoke. "I respect you," he said slowly, "and I respect your wishes . . . in spite of what you may think. It's just that—I'm very strongly attracted to you, and I'm having the devil of a time controlling it. Do you understand that?" Leah nodded gravely, ignoring the undercurrent of excitement that his words evoked. "I still want to have dinner with you tonight," he said. "And I make you a solemn vow. Nothing will happen . . . that you don't want to happen."

Somehow Leah could not find fault with what he said. She looked at him steadily. "I would like to have dinner with you," she said in a low, pleasant voice. "But not tonight. Please understand. I want to be by myself tonight and at least make a start on the work that I came here to do. It's important to me. And then . . . could you ask me again some other night this week?"

"Tomorrow night," said Taylor firmly, and Leah smiled her assent. He bent down to give her a chaste kiss on her sun-pinkened cheek. "I'll leave you in peace now. My car's waiting for me out there somewhere." He gave a wave of his arm that encompassed all the parking lots connected to the hotels along the beach.

Leah chuckled softly and lifted her fingers in fare-well as Taylor crossed the short width of the beach. She watched his back as he walked with long strides, the impressive width of his bronzed shoulders, the smooth play of muscles down his back and thighs. Just watching him in motion set off a warm stirring inside of her.

Leah moved down the beach to gather up her blanket and art supplies and carried them up the flight of stairs to her room.

Chapter Three

Another kind of excitement was building inside Leah as she entered the door to her room and set her armload of supplies down on the floor. She stood a moment, hands resting on her slim hips, and surveyed the group of blank canvases that were still ranged about the room. This was it! Tonight would be the night when she would take her career into her own hands, would perhaps set off in a new and original direction. She began to set up her work space but stopped when a gnawing in her stomach told her she had gone too long without a meal. She debated whether she should change into comfortable clothes first or delve immediately into the snacks that she had bought earlier at the nearby market, which now lay in their paper bag on the driftwood bench by the dresser.

Then something else caught her eye. The little red button on the phone was lit, signifying that there was a message waiting for her. She wondered if her mother was checking on her again so soon. It did seem unlikely. With a slight frown, she picked up the receiver and dialed the front desk.

"Hello, this is Leah DuChaine. Is there a message for me?"

"Oh, yes." The friendly voice of Joyce Becker came over the line. "A woman from the Vero Beach Art Guild came by earlier today to see you."

"Whatever for?" asked Leah in surprise.

"Well"—Joyce suddenly sounded a bit flustered— "it seems she had lunch today with a friend of mine. You see, I had told my friend—yesterday, after I talked with your mother—"

"My mother!"

"Yes, your mother called the desk yesterday afternoon to see if you had arrived safely."

"But I called her as soon as I got in!"

"Yes, dear, but she had already called the hotel once, just before you arrived. I think she was a little worried. Well, she and I got to talking—"

Leah groaned inwardly.

"—and she started telling me all about you. How talented you are and how you came to Vero Beach just to paint. She was *so* enthusiastic, and I just happened to tell a friend of mine a little bit about you. And *she* had lunch with Rhoda Hughes, the president of the art guild, today and told her about you, and Rhoda wants to meet you. I tried to call you earlier—"

"Does she want me to call her?" asked Leah reluctantly.

Joyce sighed. "I'm afraid Rhoda Hughes will be up to see you shortly."

"Right now?" asked Leah, shaking her head.

"Yes. Her car just pulled into the parking lot."

"Thank you." Leah replaced the receiver in its

cradle, then raced over to the closet and quickly pulled on some jeans and a shirt. Then she ran around the room, arranging her blank canvases in one neat stack.

Leah appreciated her mother's pride in her but did wish she would refrain from discussing her with virtual strangers. Mrs. Hughes would undoubtedly be a very nice older lady—most of the people who actually lived in Vero Beach were retirees—who doted on her grandchildren and whose taste in art ran to bright, fussy oils of daisies and fruit baskets. Why in the world would she want to talk to Leah?

The expected knock came at the door, and Leah opened it and asked her visitor to step in.

Mrs. Hughes looked as if she were in her early fifties and was not what Leah had expected. There was nothing grandmotherly about her, or perhaps she was one of the new breed of grandmothers, fit and slender and with a fashionable coiffure. The look of intelligence in her eyes caught Leah's interest. "Please call me Rhoda," she said, extending her arm to shake Leah's hand with firmness. "I do hope I'm not disturbing you."

"Not at all," murmured Leah. "Please have a seat." She made a motion toward one of the two chairs in the room.

"Oh, I won't stay long." Rhoda remained standing as she spoke. "I suppose Joyce Becker told you that I preside over the Vero Beach Art Guild. I'm always glad to meet a fellow artist—though from what I hear, you're well above the class of Sunday painters, of which I am an enthusiastic member. I understand you've been studying art in Europe for some years and have developed quite an original style."

"Well, I work in oils, and I've been doing some experimental work with glazes."

"Yes, that's what your mother told Joyce Becker."

"She did?" Leah was surprised that this information had traveled accurately from her mother to Joyce, to a friend, to Rhoda Hughes. "Please, have a seat," she insisted.

Rhoda sat on the end of the bed, and Leah sat in one of the chairs, waiting to hear if there was a concrete reason for this visit.

"I'd love to hear more about your work," urged Rhoda in her pleasant, interested voice.

"Some of it is nonrepresentational," said Leah, "but all of it derives from the very detailed realistic drawings from life which I do every day. Here . . ." She crossed the room and picked up the pad of newsprint that she had been using and held it out to Rhoda. "This is what I've been working on today."

Leah slowly flipped through the pages for the older woman to view. There were one or two close-up studies of palm fronds, so complex in patterns of light and shade that they could stand on their own as abstractions, and a sketch of a very young child sitting back on her heels, digging in the sand, her form rounded and intent; and then they came to the sketch of the girl in the bikini, standing with one hip jutting out, her arms held behind her, one hand loosely holding the other wrist, curls of sea foam reaching up to her toes.

"This is *quite* good," said Rhoda with pleasure. "How do you incorporate these studies into your paintings?"

"Occasionally, I'll use a form exactly as I sketched it," Leah explained. "More often, these drawings serve only as inspiration. Though you can't tell by the sketches, my main interest is in color. I might use colors that I remember from a particular scene, or I might use my imagination to create the color scheme."

She started to pull the sketch pad out of Rhoda's hands, but Rhoda instinctively lifted the page she was currently inspecting to glance at what was underneath. The bold yet sensitive lines of the drawing Leah had done of Taylor came partially into view.

At first, Leah tightened her grip on the sketch pad, but when she saw that Rhoda had every intention of viewing the drawing, she relinquished her hold.

"Why do you try to hide this?" the older woman asked her. "This is the best one of the lot."

"Perhaps it is," said Leah noncommittally. "I find it rather—"

"Disturbing?" asked Rhoda, giving Leah a keen-eyed look. "I wouldn't be surprised. This is a disturbingly attractive man. Do you know him well?"

A soft smile came unbidden to Leah's rosy lips as she thought of how she and Taylor had grown to know each other better earlier that afternoon. Then she shook her head. "I just met him yesterday afternoon," she said, a trace of wonder in her voice. "I really don't know him at all."

Rhoda closed up the sketch pad and handed it to Leah. "I'm glad you showed these to me," she said. "I would be thrilled to be able to see some of your paintings. In fact, I will forge ahead with my request —for I do have a request." She smiled. "The Vero Beach Art Guild is having a small showing a week from tomorrow . . ."

Leah kept her face politely blank as she listened to Rhoda Hughes's words. Surely this intelligent woman did not expect Leah to concoct a set of paintings hastily in order to beef up their local art show! What a tactless suggestion, as if Leah had nothing more pressing to do with her time than to "crank out art" to satisfy the desires of people she didn't even know.

"I anticipate your objections," said Rhoda with a smile. "Of course, if it's any inconvenience to you, please feel free to say no. And please understand that I don't feel that I'm presenting *you* with a golden opportunity. Vero Beach is a lovely town, but it's not New York, and it's obviously not the place for a promising young artist to hold an important show. I was just wondering . . . if you have a painting, or perhaps two, somewhere that you wouldn't mind exhibiting in our show . . ."

Leah's deep blue eyes were impassive.

"Let me explain that my reasons for requesting this are purely selfish," Rhoda went on. "I'm a dyed-in-the-wool art lover. I enjoy the shows that our guild sets up, and we work at keeping the quality of the pieces as high as possible. We would be thrilled to be able to exhibit one or two of your paintings. And there's something else you must know." Her eyes shone merrily. "I can understand your hesitation at showing works that may be beyond the appreciation of the general public. I understand that your work, though often representational, is very contemporary. Well, let me assure you, there is an audience in this town for your work. There are many retired people here, people who moved to Florida for the climate and relaxed life-style but who have not lost their sophisticated taste. And there are many who have the means to purchase what they admire, though I don't expect you to put your works up for sale unless you have a particular desire to do so. Why, I have many friends myself—" Rhoda broke off and laughed at the look of dawning comprehension in Leah's eyes. "Yes, you may well think that I'm asking this solely for the pleasure of a group of my cronies! Well, that's not far off the mark."

Leah found herself liking this frank woman very much indeed. Why not grant her such a simple request? "I do have two paintings at my parents' house," said Leah, "that happen to be already crated for shipping. I never got around to unpacking them when I came back from Europe."

"Marvelous!" enthused Rhoda.

"You've talked me into it," said Leah. "I would be proud to be an exhibitor in your show. I'll call my mother tonight and ask her to ship the paintings down in time for the show."

"Wonderful! And my husband and I will pay all shipping and other costs," said Rhoda firmly. She stood and extended her hand. "I thank you, and I will now be on my way."

Leah made a quick decision. "Please stay," she urged, "and have dinner with me at the hotel. I would love to talk with you some more. I had planned to be something of a recluse while I was here, but . . . that is, unless your husband is expecting you."

"Oh, no, he's out of town," said Rhoda. "I'd love to dine with you. But I insist you let me take you to my favorite restaurant—the Pearl of the Sea."

"I'd love to," said Leah. "Is it—very formal?"

"Not at all," Rhoda said, laughing. "You could go like that if you wished." She gestured at Leah's jeans. "It's just that the food is exquisite. Fresh sea food, of course."

"I do have something a little better than this to wear," said Leah with a wry smile. "I'll change right away."

Leah went into the little closet-dressing area and pulled out one of the dresses she had brought, a simple blue-gray linen sheath. With her high-heeled sandals on, she would feel quite comfortable— everyone seemed to dress casually in Florida. She recombed her hair, fastening it at the back with a half-dozen hairpins.

"I'm ready," she announced as she came back into the room.

"Then we're off."

Rhoda drove Leah several blocks, their path parallel to the shore line. She turned into a parking lot fringed with palms and banyan trees.

"The Pearl of the Sea," repeated Leah, smiling at the small, squarish wooden building that was the restaurant. They walked through the front doors and entered a room that was much more elegant than the exterior of the restaurant. The hostess led them to a table at the back, right next to a large picture window that overlooked the ocean.

"This is delightful," Leah said as they opened their menus.

"Yes, you must get your young man to bring you here some time," said Rhoda, eyes twinkling.

"My young man?"

Rhoda shrugged. "Any young man will do, I suppose. But how about that handsome one whose likeness you captured in your sketchbook? The one you barely know?"

Rhoda was laughing, but Leah couldn't take offense. Rhoda's manner was too kind and friendly for that, though her comments were a little too perceptive.

"Whatever shall I order?" asked Leah as she surveyed the menu.

"Stuffed flounder," said Rhoda promptly. "Though you wouldn't regret ordering anything that's listed."

"Stuffed flounder it is."

The dinner hour passed quickly, the two women thoroughly enjoying both the cuisine and the conversation. Their common interest in the world of art drew them together, and when Leah discovered that Rhoda had spent two months in Florence visiting friends a few years before, their topics of mutual interest became almost limitless.

"Well, my dear," said Rhoda as they finished their after-dinner coffee, "I'll take you back to your room now. You said you planned to spend your evening hard at creative work, and I know you're anxious to get started . . ."

Her words trailed off, and Leah noticed her eyebrows lift as she looked in the direction of the front door. Leah's back was to the door, so she couldn't see what Rhoda was looking at. Rhoda turned back to her hurriedly and tried to engage her attention, but it was too late. Leah took a surreptitious look over her shoulder, then blinked in astonishment.

Taylor Cambridge had just come in the door, his dark, commanding presence drawing the eyes of more than a few diners. At his side was a woman—the very same girl who had addressed him as Michael earlier that day on the beach. She was expensively and beautifully dressed in shades of beige and peach.

Taylor did not seem to notice Leah. And no wonder, she thought. I must seem drab and colorless in comparison with his date. But of course it didn't really matter. She turned back to Rhoda, who was paying the check.

When she threw another secretive look over her shoulder, she saw that Taylor had spotted her, for he was glaring intensely in her direction. Leah quickly turned back again, as if the impact of his angry look had repelled her. Was he really directing all that anger at her?

She and Rhoda got to their feet and started toward the front door of the restaurant. By that time, Taylor and his date were following the hostess to their table. Leah passed close by Taylor, and he gave her a restrained nod. She, in turn, gave him a frosty look. Sherry had brushed by her, ignoring her, and as Leah went through the front door, the flowery scent of the other girl's perfume was still strong in her nostrils.

"That bothered you, didn't it?" said Rhoda gently once they were in the car on their way back.

"You knew who that was?" asked Leah.

"Of course. Right away. The man in your sketch."

Leah heaved a trembly sigh. "There's no need for me to be upset. I barely know him."

"So you said."

"But, you see—I refused a date with him tonight."

"You did? My dear, you flatter me," said Rhoda with great good humor. Then she shook her head. "And amaze me," she said.

"Why? Just because I turned down a date with a good-looking guy?"

"No, that's not it," replied Rhoda. "It's just that—I think there's something that might be useful for you to learn."

"Which is—?"

"To go after what you want," said Rhoda firmly.

"But what do I want?" asked Leah with a shrug.

"You don't need me to tell you that," said Rhoda with a kind smile.

They turned into the parking lot of the Ocean Inn.

"Thank you for the wonderful dinner," Leah said, smiling.

"It was my pleasure. I'll be waiting with great anticipation for the arrival of your paintings."

* * *

The first thing Leah did when she entered her room was to cross over to the phone and dial her parents' number. Her mother answered, happiness in her voice.

"It's *so good* to hear your voice, Leah!"

"Mother, it's only been a day since I last talked to you!"

"I know, but somehow I can't resign myself to your absence the way I could when you were traipsing all over Europe."

Leah explained to her mother the reason for her call and asked her if she could have the paintings shipped immediately. Her mother was breathlessly excited about the art show, much more excited than Leah was, and she promised to have the paintings sent.

After hanging up the phone, Leah changed into shorts and an oversized shirt and spread newspapers on the floor, shoving a few minor articles of furniture out of the way. She got out her palette and squeezed blobs of color on its flat wood surface. She poured turpentine and linseed oil into separate cups. She opened the back door of the room so that the warm night breezes could chase away the foul-smelling fumes.

Actually, Leah was rather fond of the smells associated with her work. She associated them with hours of absorption in the enjoyable pursuit of producing beauty.

She dipped a two-inch-wide brush in the pigments on her palette and methodically began to cover one of her canvases with smooth, even strokes. This was the first stage of the painting. It began by looking quite formless, but as she worked, adding darker and lighter tones, she began to pull form out of the chaotic color

on the canvas. This took an hour; then she set it aside
to dry. It would be several weeks before she would be
able to apply the second layer of paint, which would
be more translucent. One thing she intended to do
soon was to try out a fairly new type of paint called
alkyd paint. She had an unopened box of alkyd
pigments in her burlap bag. This paint handled very
much like oils, was soft in consistency and responsive
to blending, yet its drying time was drastically less
than the time required for traditional oil paints to dry.
It would be good to be able to build up the layers of a
painting without having to wait so long for each coat
of paint to dry.

Leah set to work on one of the smaller canvases. It
was to be an *alla prima* painting—one that can be
accomplished in one sitting. She smiled at the idea,
for she rarely worked on a painting while sitting.
Much of her painting time was spent on her hands and
knees, crawling ignominiously around her canvas,
which was placed flat on the floor. Not exactly the
prescribed method, but it worked for her. The small
painting would be of the little girl squatting on the
beach. She opened her pad to the sketch and referred
to it from time to time as she worked. The color
scheme was strictly her own. She added pinks and
greens to the sand and blue and gold shadows to the
peach tones of the little girl's skin. She was pleased
with the final effect. She realized that the painting,
which was softer than her usual style, would appeal to
just about anybody.

By then, it was two-thirty in the morning. Leah
cleaned her paint cups, palette and brushes, then
slipped wearily into bed. She was satisfied with her
night's work.

For a while, her thoughts lingered on her dinner-
time conversation with Rhoda Hughes. She went over

in her mind all that they had discussed till she was at the point where Rhoda had looked up to see Taylor walking through the door. Then had come Leah's swift glance over her shoulder, which had resulted in a view of Taylor that she would never forget: daringly tall, with his strongly chiseled features, his brown eyes wandered over the room as if he were a king. She thought of the way he had glowered at her when his eyes lit upon her. How unfair! Why should he be angry at her when she was merely discussing her career with another woman, while *he* had sandwiched his time with her on the beach between time spent with a sexy blonde.

But a small voice inside her was trying to be fair about the situation. For the fact remained that he had asked her, Leah, out first. It was she who had stubbornly turned him down.

Chapter Four

Early the next morning, the phone at Leah's bedside began to ring, dragging her up from the depths of slumber. She groaned softly, glad that she had moved the phone to the night stand where she could reach it, and answered the call in a voice thick with sleep.

"Well, hello," came Taylor's deep voice. *He* was obviously wide awake, and there was an accusing edge to his greeting.

"Taylor!" Leah glanced sleepily at the clock and brushed pale, silver-blonde strands of hair out of her eyes. "Do you know what time it is?"

"It's eight o'clock," said Taylor promptly from the other end of the line. "Much of the world is up and about by this hour. I actually waited till now to call so that I wouldn't wake you."

"Why are you calling?" asked Leah in a dull voice.

"Because I'm quite angry with you," he answered.

"Then our feelings are mutual."

"You're angry with me?" demanded Taylor, his tone incredulous. "Now let's get this straight. I pursued you *ardently* yesterday, implored you to have dinner with me, you turned me down—with a fabricated excuse, I might point out—and you're angry?"

"I was . . . surprised . . . to see you with that girl."

"So," he said, "you're upset because I made another date after you refused to go out with me. It's difficult for me to see the logic . . . or the justice . . . in that."

"By the way, I didn't fabricate anything," said Leah. "I did intend to work last night. And I *did* work. But before I did, I had dinner with a woman who's very interested in art. I went straight home after we left the restaurant. And I painted *all night!*"

"All right, all right," soothed Taylor. "I can see how, to one with your ambitions, dinner with an art connoisseur would take precedence over having dinner with me. But what has *my* dinner date got to do with you—and your feelings?" he demanded.

"It just doesn't seem right," said Leah. "There you were on the beach, *pursuing* me, as you put it, not an hour after you've been with another woman, and then you rush back to that other woman as soon as . . ." She trailed off lamely. "I thought you said she had a boy friend."

"Leah, Leah," intoned Taylor. "Where did I ever get the idea that artists are broad-minded free spirits? Don't you think your way of looking at things is rather . . . provincial? Is a woman not allowed to date more than one man in a week? Or a man not permitted to date more than one woman?"

There was silence from Leah's end of the line.

"Ah, I think I understand," said Taylor softly.

"You were surprised yesterday by my passion for you—and let me assure you, passion it is. It hurts your pride that I might be the same with another woman."

"That's not exactly true," said Leah slowly. She paused. "But it's pretty close to the truth."

"Leah," said Taylor in an intense, husky whisper that sent a by-now-familiar longing through Leah's body, "I've never wanted a woman as much as I want you. I won't pretend I've been a monk. But you're head and shoulders above Sherry and the other women who—"

"Throw themselves at you?" supplied Leah.

"If you'd like to put it that way," Taylor said with a sigh. "There's so much more to you; I'm attracted to more than just your beauty. I know you don't want to make any entangling commitments. But surely there's room in your life for the kind of passion that one must share?"

"Taylor, don't you think you're going a little too fast?"

"I won't go any faster than you want me to," promised Taylor. "We'll have dinner tonight. We'll get to know each other better. I'll take you home the instant you ask me to—I hope not before we share a few kisses."

"That sounds harmless enough."

"Harmless!" growled Taylor. "Leah, you insult me! I'll come over there and show you how harmless—"

"I haven't even gotten out of bed yet!"

"In that case, I'll be over right away."

"Don't you dare!"

"Dinner, then," said Taylor. "I'll pick you up at seven. If I can wait that long."

After Leah hung up the phone, she luxuriated in her bed, her hands crossed behind her head. A soft smile curved her lips, and her blue eyes shone dreamily.

Passion. He had used the word easily, in a way that made her wonder. She had made a firm decision that she would not involve herself permanently with any man. But was Taylor correct in his observation that pleasure—passion—could still be a part of her life?

A warm, delicious aching spread throughout her body. She shifted her head uneasily on her pillow, her hair spilling about her face in shining curves. It was both delightful and infuriating, this longing that swept over her when she thought of Taylor or heard his voice or felt his caress. But there was another emotion mingled with these two, a cold, hard feeling that it took a few moments for her to identify.

It was fear. Undeniable, icy-fingered fear, which dampened her pleasure and constricted her heart. She tried to consider it disinterestedly. Was she afraid of abandoning herself to the passion that was promised in Taylor's eyes? Or was it something else she was afraid of—perhaps the dangers to her career that she perceived?

Now thoroughly awake, she got out of bed and pulled on her customary casual clothes, then set out for a long, vigorous walk down the beach. She started off in the direction opposite the one that she and Taylor had taken the previous day. She breathed deeply of the warm salty air and seemed to take in strength with each inhalation. The crashing waves sent emissaries to the shore, foamy wavelets that curled about her ankles. Dozens of sandpipers skittered across the sand, first rushing bravely toward the sea, then turning to retreat frantically from the waves through which Leah boldly splashed.

Thoroughly refreshed, she turned back to the hotel.

She made a quick trip to the nearby market and bought a loaf of bread, a thick slab of cheese and a bag of oranges. She planned to keep them in her room and subsist on them as far as was possible in order to economize. She still had a sizable sum of money left from three commissions her art teacher had helped her procure while in Florence, but she wanted to extend her period of financial freedom for as long as possible. She knew she had been very fortunate in money matters, beginning with the legacy from a wealthy great-aunt that had enabled her to go to Europe and continuing with the fees for commissions she had executed while in Italy. Still, her money wouldn't last indefinitely, and she didn't plan to squander it on nonessentials that meant little to her.

She spent another morning sketching under the sun on the beach. As usual, she attracted several onlookers who made admiring comments and drifted on.

It was not uncommon for Leah to become so engrossed in her work that she would allow one or two meal times to slip by without even realizing she was hungry. But today, as the sun drew high overhead, she became very aware of the emptiness of her stomach. She decided to bring her food out to one of the umbrella-shaded tables on the patio of her hotel and enjoy lunch in the open air.

A waiter approached as she settled herself at a table and inquired if there was something he could bring her. She asked for a glass of white wine, which he brought a few minutes later. One of the things Leah had acquired after two years in Europe was the habit of drinking wine with her meals. She ate leisurely.

The waiter later brought the bill for the wine, and she bent her head as she signed it. She handed it back to him with a smile and a tip; then, as she turned her head, she saw Taylor standing a few feet away from her table, his brown eyes glowing.

She was not surprised to see him there, only as pleased as she could be at the sight of his tall, well-muscled body and his friendly, expectant smile. He wore a green knit shirt and bright white shorts that contrasted sharply with the darkly tanned skin of his thighs.

"May I join you?" he asked.

"Is it seven already?" asked Leah in mock puzzlement.

"Oh, come now. I told you I wouldn't be able to wait," he said, pulling out a chair. "How about having a wine cooler with me?"

"If I keep drinking wine, I'll be asleep by seven," she said.

"I knew you were a lot of fun," he teased. "Come on. One cooler won't hurt you."

He beckoned to the waiter, who soon arrived with two tall icy glasses.

"This is delicious," she said as the cool, sweet liquid trickled down her throat.

Taylor covered her hand with his. "I hope you're looking forward to tonight as much as I am," he said. "I thought we might go to Jason's. It's not a showy place, but it's got the finest lobster you've ever sunk your teeth into."

"It sounds wonderful. I didn't think I would be dining out so much when I came down here. First there was my meal last night, and now tonight . . . I really thought I would spend my entire time here in jeans and bathing suits!"

"Why don't you let me buy you a dress to wear tonight?" he suggested. "There are some shops across the street—"

"Good heavens, no!" she blurted out. "I've got something I'm sure will be suitable."

"I don't doubt that," he said with surprise. "But I've never known a woman who wouldn't be excited at the prospect of a pretty new dress."

There was a trace of scorn in Leah's laugh. "Perhaps you haven't," she said, "but there are people, you know, who would not consider accepting an expensive gift from a man they've just met."

Taylor's expression was almost unreadable, but there was a shadow of displeasure in his eyes. "You're right about the women I know," he said slowly. "Most of them have no compunctions at all along those lines."

"Does that have anything to do with your trick of using an alias when you introduce yourself to women?" she asked lightly.

Taylor's mouth twitched. "If you knew the whole story, I don't think you'd condemn me for it."

Leah silently sipped her cooler.

"Leah, I go by the name of Michael Slayton very seldom." Taylor's dark gaze was intent. "But I wonder if you can imagine what it's like to be introduced to someone, and suddenly you realize that they know much more about you than you do about them—that they have a pretty good idea of what you're worth, that they know the restaurants you frequent and who goes with you, that they've read reports of your activities and your statements, accurate or not. And then you can see that they're not really interested in you, but only in what you can give them—and that they're willing to do almost anything they think would win your favor, whether you ask them to or not."

"I admit, it doesn't sound too pleasant. It would make me very nervous." Leah was watching Taylor with real interest. "Tell me. Do you use your alias with men, too, or only with women?"

"Sometimes with men," he said, smiling, "if I go out to have a few drinks, and I want to join in the general conversation without being regarded as somebody special. Sometimes it doesn't work, though, because my photograph has been published upon occasion."

"What different worlds we come from," she mused. "I'm sure I seem quite unsophisticated to you."

"No," he said, shaking his head, "you seem wonderful to me. And not so unsophisticated as all that. Didn't your parents send you to Europe to study art at the age when many girls are working or settling down to have babies?"

By this time, the rest of the patio seemed to have receded from around them till all that existed was the umbrella-shaded table over which they conversed intimately. Leah found that her usual reticence had evaporated, leaving a willingness to talk freely of what was often on her mind.

"My mother and father didn't send me to Europe," she said. "They couldn't have, not without help." She took a deep breath. "You see, I had a legacy—from my great-aunt, who died when I was twenty-one. She had taken my sister out of her will, much to Eve's surprise. I suppose she felt that Eve didn't need any more money. My mother and father certainly could have used part of my inheritance, and I offered it, but"—her fingers were tracing patterns on the side of her frosty glass—"my mother insisted I use it all to further my career. She was the one who wanted me to study abroad—even though she knew it would bring her sorrow to see her second daughter go so far away. That's part of why I feel I owe her so much. I've got to succeed—I can't let her down."

Taylor's expression was serious. "Guilt hardly seems a good motivation for pursuing a career," he said.

"It's not guilt that motivates me," she said quietly. "The love of creating is my basic motivation. But I do think of my mother a lot. The discipline I impose on myself is made easier by thinking of all she's done for me. And if she wants to see her own dreams come true through me—well, is there really anything wrong with that?"

"Was your mother an artist, too?"

"She could have been," she said. "But then she fell in love."

Taylor chuckled. "You make that sound like it was a serious mistake."

"It was," said Leah vehemently, but then a smile touched her lips. "Apparently, my father was irresistible. Of course, I love him, too. But sometimes I wonder if my mother would have married, had she known what it would mean for her. She had to work part-time to help make ends meet. She kept house. She raised her children. There was not much time left for painting. She and my father are still in love—but even so, I know she feels a sense of loss. She did find time to encourage both of her daughters to develop their talent. If we hadn't been born with it, I'm sure mother would have found a way to inject it into us!"

"She must be proud of your dedication and your hard work. Many people don't believe in those things anymore."

Leah looked at him. "*You* must work hard," she said. "Doesn't it take a lot of work to manage your business?"

"I do work hard," he agreed. "But I didn't start with nothing. My great-grandfather opened our family's first department store eighty years ago . . ."

Leah tapped the table top suddenly with her finger tips. "So that's who you are!" she said. "Cambridge Payne!" Cambridge Payne was a deluxe department store that catered to an exclusive clientele. It had originated in New York but had branched out into other domestic and foreign cities. "Do you own it?"

Taylor nodded. "My family does. I serve as president of the corporation, and my father is chairman of the board. Geoffrey Payne sold out a generation ago, so it's completely in our family now." He reflected a moment. "Yes, I believe in hard work, too." He gave her a direct look. "But I also believe in enjoying the fruits of one's labors, in taking the finest life has to offer."

Leah said nothing.

Taylor touched her hand again. "I'd like to continue our conversation tonight," he said. "Over dinner."

"Yes, I believe it's time to work on my painting," she said.

"Just for a change of pace?" he teased. They rose, and he gave her a brief, gentle kiss. Leah tilted back her head to receive it as if it were the most natural thing in the world. "I'll be back here at seven," he said. He gave her a wink. "If not before then."

The afternoon passed slowly for Leah. She was not as pleased with her work as she might have been. By quarter to six, she was already stepping into her white silk dress. She knew full well that Taylor might show up early, and she intended to be ready when he arrived. She slid the zipper up the back of her dress, thinking as she did so that the dress was unusually elegant for her—it had been a gift from her sister. It was close fitting, with a moderately low neckline and a flaring hem. Though it was becoming, Leah had seldom worn it. She had decided to bring it at the last minute just so she would have more than one dress to choose from.

She looked at the floor of the closet. Her white high-heeled sandals would have to do.

She put on a touch more makeup than was her habit. She brushed her hair with many strokes till it shone in a silky curtain about her shoulders. Taylor would like that, she was sure. But then, perhaps out of habit, she pulled her hair back from her face, twisted it and secured it with pins.

It was now quarter after six.

Leah stepped out onto the back deck and waved to a man who was fitting his key into the lock of his door several rooms away. She sat and waited in one of the rocking chairs, hands folded in her lap.

Don't be silly, she chided herself. *It's not even close to seven yet.*

But she grew tired of waiting and wandered down to the soft drink machine. She carried her drink back upstairs to the deck and sipped it thoughtfully as she waited.

At precisely seven, she heard a car pull into the parking lot, a door slam, then a man's footsteps coming up the stairs. She rose, and Taylor stood before her in a finely tailored cream-colored linen suit and a blue shirt, a rakish smile on his face.

"You came."

"Of course, you little idiot." But the warmth of his kiss gave the lie to his words. Already her senses were swimming, and the evening had barely begun. Lightly, she pressed her body against his.

"Hold it now; we'll never get away from here if this keeps up. Here, let me see that great dress."

Leah stood back so he could look at her and felt a

warm flush sting her cheeks as his eyes ravished her from head to toe.

"Let's go, beautiful," he said, and they went down the stairs and out to his waiting car.

"You really shouldn't try to hide your figure," he said as he perused the wine list, "with those jeans and baggy T-shirts you wear."

"Do you often make such personal comments?" Leah inquired. "Believe me, I don't try to *hide* anything. I just like to be comfortable. I can't imagine wearing a silk dress while painting with oils and turpentine."

"I find the image quite appealing," said Taylor with a grin. "But you do have a point. Perhaps that's the best reason for going out to places like this, so you can have a chance to show me your oh-so-beautiful curves!" He raised his eyebrows humorously.

"Really, Taylor!" she chastised. "I can think of better reasons for going out than that!"

"You can?"

"Yes, food for one!"

"You disappoint me, Leah," he said, shaking his head. "How can you think of food at a time like this! Oh, well, if you must."

The restaurant was attractively paneled in dark wood, its corners softened with gracefully draped netting. Snowy linens covered the table tops, low candles glimmered on each table, and the tableware was pewter and blue-and-white pottery. The effect was one of casual elegance with a faintly maritime air.

Taylor ordered a bottle of Pouilly-Fuissé; the wine steward brought it to their table, filled their glasses and left.

Taylor lifted his glass. "To you," he said simply, and brought the glass to his lips.

They dined on salad and lobster, both of which were excellent. When the meal was over, the waiter brought them coffee, and they talked awhile over the fragrant steaming cups.

"Tell me about your sister," suggested Taylor. "Is she anything like you?"

Leah would have been happy just to gaze in silence into Taylor's warm brown eyes, but he was attentive and genuinely interested, and again she felt encouraged to talk.

"I used to think she was like me," Leah said with a half smile. "She's three years older than I am. She was a dedicated artist, a water-colorist. Six years ago, when she was twenty-two, she met an older man. He was thirty-five at the time."

"Does that seem so old to you?" asked Taylor. "I'm almost thirty-five myself."

"It was quite an age difference, yes, especially for a twenty-two-year-old just out of college! He simply swept her off her feet. They were married six months after they met." She paused. "She hasn't painted a picture since."

"So history repeated itself," he commented. "And does she work and raise her children and clean the house as your mother did?"

"No, her story is quite different. Her husband had a lot of material benefits to offer her—he owns an oil company. He showers her with jewelry and furs. She wants for nothing. She has one child and can afford plenty of household help."

"And yet she gave up her painting."

"Yes. Her husband wouldn't have minded if she had kept it up. It was just that she couldn't resist the temptations of the new life he offered her— entertaining, shopping, accompanying him when he traveled on business trips. My father is delighted that

Eve seems so happy, but I think my mother under-stands the empty areas in Eve's life."

"And you think there is emptiness?"

"Oh, yes," said Leah emphatically. "I know that Eve would trade all her designer dresses, servants and jewels for a few excellent paintings that she herself had done. If only she had the will to carry it through . . ." Leah thought a moment. "The sad part is that Eve made such a marriage at least partially because she didn't want to be a burden on our parents. I know she loves Jerry, and she does have her own pleasures in her life. But I also know that she took our family's financial situation into account when she decided to marry a wealthy man. She's generous to a fault. She loves to give us surprise gifts. Jerry gave her a new car a few months ago, and she passed her old car, that Volvo, along to me. She loves to give."

"But the things she has in her life—" Taylor was watching her with concentrated attention. "The beau-tiful clothes, the leisure, the social life—these things have no value in your eyes?"

"Very little," said Leah with a shrug. "There are things worth much more than a life-style like Eve's." She was aware as she spoke that she was sending Taylor a powerful message; she could see by his thoughtful expression that he had understood her message very well.

Taylor called for the check and paid the bill. "Well, shall we go?"

Leah nodded.

They walked out the front door into the parking lot, into the warm Florida night air. Leah was struck by the unusual shapes of the palms and the banyan trees in the darkness and the scent of the hibiscus. Another couple was getting out of their car on the far side of the parking lot, but Taylor ignored them and pulled Leah to one side under a darkened palm and gathered her into his arms. His kiss was gently insistent, and she seemed to melt into him in response. He was reluctant to let her go, but the other couple brushed past them, the man saying with amusement, "Excuse me, sir." Taylor released her with a grin and led her to the car.

"Now what shall it be?" asked Taylor, his arms resting on the steering wheel. "A short drive, a walk on the beach, a late movie—or maybe you'll let me show you my beach house?"

"I'd love to see your house," said Leah, but she grew a trifle apprehensive at the warm, delighted look he gave her.

They drove for several miles along the coast, then turned into a drive that led to an imposing frame house with majestic lines and lit by many exterior lights. Leah's surprise showed clearly on her face.

"This is your little beach cottage?" she asked.

"I never said it was a cottage," he said, smiling. "You may be glad to know we have a chaperone tonight. The Nelsons are a couple who work for me and take care of the house when I'm gone. Nelson is here this evening, though his wife is out visiting relatives."

They walked up the poinsettia-lined path, and the front door seemed to open of its own accord.

"You were watching for us, eh, Nelson?" Taylor chuckled as he guided Leah inside.

Nelson was a middle-aged man, casually dressed as befitted the climate, but he seemed to be a model of efficiency. "There's some wine chilling in the sunroom, Mr. Cambridge," said Nelson. "As you requested."

Leah threw Taylor a sharp glance, wondering if he had been certain that she would accompany him back to his house.

"I like to be prepared for all possibilities." Taylor shrugged, and Leah laughed.

Nelson withdrew, and Leah tried to take everything in as Taylor led her to the rear of the house. She was struck by the subtle good taste in the furnishings and the wealth that it implied. It could be called a casual beach house, yes, but it was beautifully designed, with airy rooms and interesting wall coverings, and the furnishings were carefully selected. Most of the furniture was of oiled teak, some inlaid with beautiful Scandinavian tiles in cream, blue and brown. The upholstered pieces were covered in fine natural fabrics, the carpeting was plush and chocolate colored, and the walls displayed a collection of contemporary art that caught Leah's eye.

"Who built this lovely house?" she asked. "And who collected the art?"

"An architect friend of mine designed the house, and two women who work for me furnished it and selected the art. The art buyer, Polly, despairs of this location for all her finds, but we had them framed so that they would withstand the humid climate."

"And is the architect a woman, too?" she asked, not knowing why she asked.

"Yes, she is," he replied. "Come, let me show you the sunroom."

The sunroom was spacious and enclosed with glass on three sides, its corners crowded with cacti and potted palms that duplicated the vegetation to be found outdoors. The floor was white tile and the furniture natural-colored wicker except for the long coffee-colored sofa that lined the inner wall. The sliding doors in the back overlooked the ocean, and Taylor now crossed the room and opened them wide to let in the sea air.

"May I pour you some wine?" he asked, glancing at the bottle that was chilling in an ice bucket.

"Thank you, no," Leah answered, settling back into one corner of the couch. She tilted her head back, gazing at the stars, which could be seen dimly through the skylights.

"Here, I'll turn out the lights so you can really see the stars." Taylor flicked a switch, and the room fell into semidarkness, lit only by the lights that remained on in the front of the house. Leah heard the faint pop of a cork and a bubbling liquid sound as Taylor poured himself a glass of wine. He settled his long form on the couch beside Leah and gave a contented sigh.

"Are you sure you won't join me in a glass of wine?" he asked again.

Leah's head remained tilted back, resting on the high edge of the sofa as she looked through the skylight. "I've had too much wine today," she said slowly, "and I'm almost too relaxed." She raised her head and turned to face him in the shadows.

Taylor gave a soft chuckle and gently rubbed her shoulder with the back of his hand. "Don't tell me you feel you're in any danger," he said half humorously.

"Oh, but I am in danger, am I not?" she returned.

She had tried to make her tone light and teasing, but she saw by Taylor's face that he had caught the vague disquiet that accompanied her words. He withdrew his hand, straightened up for a moment and set his glass down on a nearby table with a muffled click.

"Leah," he said, "this is important. You realize you're here of your own free will."

"Of course," she said, surprised.

He reached for her hand and quietly closed his

fingers over hers. "I've wanted you here with me, Leah, for the last two days. I thought there was something special about you when I first saw you. I was right." His dark eyes burned into her, forcing her to return his gaze. His voice grew husky. "I want you, Leah."

The intensity in his voice caused a pleasurable jolt within her. Now that the moment was there, she wondered if she was prepared for it.

She had known the moment would come, had known it after Taylor's morning phone call, had known it when she agreed to come with him to his house after dinner. All day she had debated with herself in an attempt to decide what she would do when the moment arrived. "There's room in your life for passion," he had said to her over the phone that morning, and in her mind she thought she could almost accept the idea of pleasure without commitment. But something deeply rooted inside her had rebelled against the idea. Some very important part of her believed that the idea was wrong. She didn't know what part of her it was—perhaps her own timidity, perhaps a true moral sense. But her intellect had proved very persuasive, too, and combined with the powerful longings of her body, in the end, it triumphed.

She leaned almost imperceptibly toward Taylor, her head slightly tilted. He did not touch her with his hands at first, but began to cover her face with slow kisses. When he pressed his mouth to hers, he found her eager to respond.

His hands tightly clenched her shoulders as he tasted her lips. "Delicious," he murmured, and she smiled through their kiss.

She put her arms around him, and her hands slid up his back, stroking the powerful, flexing muscles of his shoulders. He drew back to loosen his tie, pulled it off and tossed it on the floor. Hastily, he unbuttoned his shirt, shrugged it off, and it followed the tie to the floor.

His arms engulfed her, and she gasped as her body was drawn intimately against the curly mat on his broad chest. Her body was alive with sensation, from the rough contact of the linen sofa on her back and the silky feel of the dress that clung to her to the taste of his hard masculine lips that devoured her in another intoxicating kiss.

The kiss ended, and Taylor looked at her through eyes half closed with desire. Then, with slow-moving hands, he removed the pins from her hair and watched the pale blonde strands tumble down.

"You should always wear it that way," he muttered; then he buried his fingers in her hair and his mouth in her soft, fragrant neck.

An irresistible wave of desire washed over Leah as she felt the heat of his hard male body and the urgency of his demands. And sweet desire banished all troublesome thoughts and uncertainties from her mind.

Soft cries of pleasure escaped her as he explored her shoulders, throat and upper chest with his mouth. She sank back farther against the couch under his relentless advance. "Not afraid, are you?" he whispered, and she shook her head.

He crushed the white silk of her dress as he stroked her upper body feverishly, then slipped his hands beneath her shoulders. She raised her body slightly to allow him to reach the zipper in the back of the dress, and he slid it smoothly open to her waist. Then she lay quietly, breathing unsteadily, as he pulled the dress off her shoulders and down to her waist to reveal the glowing satin of her skin, her smooth bare shoulders, the rounded fullness of her breasts.

"Ah, let me just look at you," he said hoarsely, and half rose as if to go turn on the light, then thought better of it. "No, I can't leave you," he said with a sigh, and he reached for her breasts.

Leah moaned in restless pleasure, clutching at his muscular shoulders. Taylor slid his hands down to her waist and pressed his upper body insistently against hers, as if to impress upon her the differences between their bodies. She twisted gently beneath him, feeling almost burned by the hot kisses he showered on her throat. Mindlessly, she scraped his back with her finger tips.

His breathing grew more ragged as he devoured her softness with his tongue and lips. Maintaining their meltingly close contact, he began to tug the close-fitting dress down over her hips.

It was at this moment that Leah began to resist. Though every powerful physical instinct instructed her to yield to him, some part of her that she had tried to bury began to scream silently, *I'm not ready for this.* Her body tensed convulsively, and gasping, she struggled against Taylor with all her strength.

"What the hell's the matter!" he demanded roughly. Dazed, he started to relinquish his hold on her. Then he tightened his grasp once again, and for a moment she thought that he would try to proceed in spite of her struggles. But he let her go and sat back heavily on the sofa.

"There's a name for women like you," he said in a deadly voice. "I can understand it happening once, but I didn't think it would get to be a habit." He made no move to put his shirt back on, but sat unblinking, watching Leah as she thrust her arms through the sleeves of her dress and struggled with the zipper. It seemed to be caught on something; she could not budge it, and tears of frustration started to her eyes.

"Here, I'll do that," Taylor offered. "No, don't give me that look. I won't be tempted to molest you. If I could stop myself the way I did just then, I can do anything."

Efficiently, he closed the zipper, then motioned her to sit down on the couch again. He moved back a little to allow more space between them.

"Now—tell me what came over you."

"I'm sorry," said Leah contritely, pushing her hair back from her face. "I didn't mean for that to happen. I guess I . . . in spite of my brave intentions, I just can't go through with it."

"What the hell's stopping you?" he exploded. He jerked to his feet and began to pace, his shoulders gleaming in the subdued light.

Leah stared at him.

"You're a virgin, aren't you!" Taylor snapped, and he made it sound like an accusation.

"What does that have to do with it!" demanded Leah, angry at herself because she knew she sounded defensive.

"How could a beautiful woman your age— Oh, yes, I know. You've been much too busy." He continued to pace, and as he did, Leah saw some of the tension leave his body. He came to a stop in front of her and lifted her small chin with his strong fingers. A look of tenderness replaced the frustration in his eyes. "Well, I'm chalking this one up to *lack* of experience," he said gently. "Yours."

Leah tried to swallow the lump in her throat. "It's not just lack of experience," she said in a whisper. "I don't think that it's possible for me to have—what you want—without some kind of commitment."

Taylor gave an ironic laugh. "And yet you're the one who intends to avoid a permanent relationship at all costs."

"I know." Leah looked down at the floor.

Taylor stepped back and sat on the wicker chair facing her. He leaned forward, hands clasped, elbows resting on his knees, and regarded her seriously.

"Leah, I'm leaving for New York early tomorrow morning," he said. "I'm going to be very busy with the store. I plan to be gone about a week. At the end of that time, I'll come back to Vero Beach. And if you're still here, we can talk. I think we'll have a lot to talk about."

"You mean you want to see me again?" Leah's voice expressed her astonishment.

"Of course, you little idiot," said Taylor, putting on his shirt and jacket. "And you'll have a little time to decide if you want to see *me* again. And now I'd better take you home. Unless, of course, you would consider staying overnight in an extremely comfortable beach house?"

Smiling, Leah shook her head, glad that Taylor had so soon regained his teasing manner.

"I thought as much," he said, guiding her toward the front door. "More's the pity."

Chapter Five

"Careful now!"

Rhoda Hughes and Leah stood together in the parking lot in front of a low whitewashed building. They were supervising two men who were unloading two large and unwieldy crates from their van. The crates contained the paintings that Leah's mother had sent down in time for the art show.

The white building was the meeting place for the Vero Beach Art Guild and housed the gallery where the current art show was to be held. It was an ugly, featureless building, its only exterior beauties being the live oaks that were scattered about it and the trumpet vines that climbed the fence that surrounded the parking lot.

Rhoda stood, hands on her hips, not hesitating to call out warnings to the perspiring men. Leah stood relaxed and observant in black jeans and white T-shirt, wayward strands from her blonde twist blowing in the warm subtropical wind.

"If you'll carry them inside for us," Rhoda said to the men, "we can manage the rest."

They all walked into the building and into a large empty room. The men set the two paintings on the floor and left.

An older man with white hair and a kindly smile ambled into the room. He was wearing a short-sleeved flowered shirt and was carrying a fistful of tools.

"Need some help?" he asked. Rhoda introduced him to Leah as Willie Polk. He set about prying open the crates.

"I'm so excited," said Rhoda. "I can hardly wait to see what you've brought us."

"I'd like to see the work of some of the other artists," said Leah.

"Some of my paintings are in the front room," said Willie quickly, with an enthusiasm that made Leah smile. "Why don't you go take a look? I won't need your help till we start to hang the paintings."

Leah walked in the direction he indicated and came to a room whose walls were covered with water colors. She looked for the paintings that bore Willie's signature. All of them were seascapes executed with extreme realism, and all bore some resemblance to most of the other works hung on the walls. Leah liked the fact that these amateur artists had found a means for creative expression and that many of them had achieved a high level of proficiency.

She rejoined Willie and Rhoda, and Willie beamed at the admiring comments Leah made about his paintings.

By this time, Leah's paintings were out of their

crates, and Rhoda had leaned them against a wall. Rhoda studied them for a few minutes, then said softly, "I knew they'd be wonderful."

One of the large paintings was done in browns and beiges with touches of cool pink and vivid blue. It was semiabstract; one could discern various human forms, all in sinuous motion. The other was a seascape, though very different from those painted by Willie Polk. It was inspired by the Mediterranean, its colors were clear and true, and it was dominated by a great expanse of sky.

"We'll hang them on this wall," declared Rhoda, "so they will be the first things people see when they enter the room. There are a couple of other artists whose work is rather unusual, and we'll hang them on the other walls of this room."

Carefully, the three hung the paintings, stepping backward to view, moving forward to adjust. Finally, they were in place.

"Magnificent," pronounced Rhoda. "And Leah, this building *is* burglarproof."

"The thought of somebody burgling my paintings never entered my mind!" Leah said, laughing.

Rhoda glanced at her watch. "Shall we lunch together?" she asked.

Willie said his wife was expecting him for lunch, so Rhoda and Leah locked up the building and climbed into Rhoda's car.

"I'd like to try lunch at the Ocean Inn," said Rhoda, "but you're probably tired of it by now."

"I certainly am not!" said Leah. "In fact, I haven't ordered a real lunch there yet!"

They planned to eat outside on the patio, but by the time they pulled into the hotel's parking lot, large drops of rain were falling from the sky. A mighty crack of thunder and black clouds that billowed onto the scene heralded the arrival of a menacing thunderstorm. They ran to the restaurant, just in time to take cover from the deluge.

They took their places at a table in the room, which was now darkened by the fury outside. They had a clear view out the back window of bathers rushing madly to gather up their paraphernalia and run for cover.

The lights flickered, and Rhoda told Leah that it was quite common for the electricity to go out during such wild storms.

"The storm season is from June to September," she said. "And there's always a hurricane somewhere across the state. We get used to it."

They engaged in pleasant conversation for most of the meal; then the topic that was uppermost in Leah's mind was brought up—by Rhoda.

"And have you seen your handsome model again?" she asked.

"Yes, I saw him several nights ago," said Leah. "He's left the state now. Gone back to New York."

"What a shame."

Leah shrugged.

"Well, you miss him, don't you?" asked Rhoda.

Leah took a deep breath. "He's only been gone for two days," she said. "And I can't think of anything but him. I just don't understand it."

"What's not to understand?" asked Rhoda with humor.

"Well, you see, I put him off again," said Leah. "It's not that I didn't have a right to refuse . . . what he was asking. My *timing* was a bit off, perhaps." A rueful smile appeared on her lips as the previous night's scene with Taylor flashed into her mind. "But why do I reject him—and then, when he leaves, I can't get him out of my mind? That's not love, is it?" she asked, half-serious.

"It could be," answered Rhoda. "I don't know. I would say you certainly are infatuated."

"Infatuation." Leah pronounced the word slowly. "What in the world do I do about that?"

"Do you want to get over it?"

"Yes, I think I do."

"Then," said Rhoda, "you either need to cut him out of your mind and life completely *or* spend more time with him—get to know him better than you do. Perhaps familiarity will breed contempt, your infatuation will disappear, and you won't be yearning after something you will have learned doesn't exist."

"And if it does exist—I suppose that's another problem entirely," mused Leah.

That night, as on the previous nights, Leah painted. Her absorption in her work helped to erase thoughts of Taylor from her mind: thoughts of his smile, his dark eyes, his powerful but graceful movements, his firm, warm lips, his gentle caresses, his rough, arousing ones. She knew she didn't really expect him to come back to Vero Beach—at least not for the sole purpose of seeing her. She would be unable to put into practice Rhoda's second suggestion for exorcizing him from her mind. The only other option was to forget him.

At times, when Leah's work was going well, she could get by on very little sleep. On that particular night, the dawn was sending its gentle glow over the ocean before she thought to lay her brushes aside. She tumbled into bed to catch a two-hour nap before she rose for the day. She was satisfied with her work of the previous few nights. She had finished one painting, and three others were in various stages of completion.

After a short sleep she rose, nibbled on a hard roll, then changed into her bathing suit. She spent an hour or so dozing on the beach. Then she went back up to her balcony to sit in the rocking chair, to look out over the ocean and to think.

Finally, she roused herself from her reverie and went down to her car. She intended to make an early appearance at the gallery, for this was the first day of the art show.

When she got to the white building that held the gallery, Rhoda was there to meet her.

"People have been streaming in!" she said. "Would you care to come to 'your' room and listen to some of the comments?"

"I've always been nervous about doing that," Leah said, smiling, "but it doesn't sound like a bad idea. That is, if I can steel myself for the criticisms."

She had priced her paintings at the upper end of the scale, not really expecting to sell them. She was shocked when Rhoda told her that her seascape had been sold not two hours after the show had opened.

Rhoda introduced her to the man who had bought her painting. She was surprised by his appearance. He looked unprepossessing with his walking shorts, glasses and his round, balding head. He certainly did not look like a man who was in the habit of impulsively spending a fortune on a work of art.

"I'm so glad to meet the artist," he said, his blue eyes shining. He had to look up at Leah, for he was several inches shorter than she was. "I must say, you're not at all what I had pictured. I was sure you were a man, a young man with long hair and a morose expression. A tormented genius, you know. Of course, that was before I saw your signature."

Leah let the laughter bubble forth. "I was just thinking that you didn't fit my image of a spendthrift connoisseur."

"Oh, this wonderful shirt put you in doubt as to the merits of my taste?" he asked, his eyebrows raised humorously as he glanced down at his gaudy printed shirt. "I'll have you know that underneath these chartreuse flowers beats the heart of a truly discerning collector."

"I didn't doubt your taste for a minute," protested Leah, and she bantered with the lively old man for an enjoyable few minutes.

After a while, Leah had had enough of the show and took her leave. She was in a good mood, because of the admiring comments she had heard on her work, the friendly people she had met and, of course, the big sale. Her savings had been dwindling slowly but steadily, and the sudden influx of funds would give her great freedom when it came time for her to decide what her next step would be.

She dozed lightly on the beach that afternoon, lack of sleep having finally taken its toll. After a light supper, she settled back into work.

She lost all awareness of time as she became engrossed in what she was doing. This night, she was applying a delicate layer of glazes to a painting that was almost finished. She was aware of nothing as she worked but her immediate surroundings, the heavy silence, the slow beating of her own heart. Her concentration was complete.

The ringing of the phone was such a startling, grating sound that for a moment Leah froze. It rang a second time, a brazen intrusion on her solitude.

On the third ring, she picked up the receiver with a soft "Hello?"

"Leah."

The voice was expressionless, but the deep tones were unmistakably his, and Leah's heart began to pound.

"Hello, Taylor," she said faintly. Then, regaining her composure, she said, "This is Taylor Cambridge, I presume?"

"Leah, there's a reason why I'm calling," he said, ignoring her flippancy. "I'm really relieved to hear your voice."

"You are?"

"Yes, I was afraid you might have gone by now. That's the reason for my call. I plan to come back to Vero in a few days—but only if you're still there." There was a question in his voice.

"Yes, I plan to be here for a while. Oh, Taylor"— she lost her bit of reserve and allowed the enthusiasm to creep in—"you'll never guess what happened today! A very nice man bought one of my paintings. He liked it so much, and he paid me quite a bit for it. It's going to make things easier for me—"

"That's wonderful!" Taylor sounded truly delighted. "That's what I'd really like to see for you: success and more success. And I know you can do it. You're the kind of person who will reach her goals."

For a moment, Leah was speechless. She was touched by Taylor's sincere encouragement, having not really expected it.

"That's very nice of you to say so," she said with a touch of formality.

"So you'll be there when I come," Taylor persisted.

"I will be here."

"Great. I'll see you in a few days, then."

And then he hung up, leaving Leah holding a buzzing phone receiver, shaking her head in puzzlement. Her contact with Taylor had come without warning, and suddenly it was gone. As she picked up

her brush to resume her work, the silence that closed
in on her seemed to be trying to convince her that she
had only imagined the call. But she had heard his
voice; he had told her that he would not come back
unless *she* were there, that she was the reason he had
called.

*Now I can spend some time with him so that I'll
grow to feel contempt for him,* said Leah to herself,
but she was smiling as she thought it.

The next few days passed in pleasant monotony.
Leah returned to the show only once, but she heard
from Rhoda and others that it was successful and that
people were talking excitedly about her work. Rhoda
remarked on Leah's calm acceptance of the comments
that were reported to her. "If I were you, I'd be a bit
more *thrilled,*" chided Rhoda.

At unexpected moments, an aching yearning would
come over Leah's body, and Taylor once again would
take possession of her mind. For the most part,
however, she was able to push thoughts of him to one
side and wait serenely for the day he was to return.

Until the day of his return. Then, that morning, she
began to feel nervous and ill at ease, and she spent the
morning in her room. She wondered if her nervousness was due to her fear that he really would not
return. She was upset with herself because it seemed
to matter so much.

Chapter Six

Leah picked up the ringing phone, knowing with a burst of gladness that it would be Taylor.

"So you made it!" she said breezily. "Or"—a sudden thought struck her—"are you still in New York?"

"Now, Leah," Taylor replied, the trace of familiar amusement in his voice, "I didn't tell you I'd try to make it back or that I *might* come back—"

"You said you *would* come back," finished Leah.

"Right. Listen, I'll try to make it over this evening. We'll have dinner, all right?"

"All . . . right," said Leah, staring as the phone went dead. Could he really mean that he would wait that long to see her? He must have something very important to do during the afternoon.

Fifteen minutes later, he was knocking at her back door. She swung it open and looked up at him, at the grin on his devastatingly handsome face.

Despite her fantasies of falling into his arms upon seeing him, she stood tentatively. But he was having none of that. He gathered her into his arms and lifted her up off the floor with the strength of his embrace. Then he kissed her, but it was a brief kiss, almost restrained.

"Come on. Let's go sit on the patio with some drinks and talk," he invited.

"You don't want to come in for a minute?"

"You can't be serious! I don't trust myself to be alone with you. You know, I haven't been with another woman since I left Vero. And it's only because my mind was on you."

Leah was taken aback by this unsolicited bit of information. She was not sure what the proper response was. Did he think she should feel flattered that thoughts of her had kept him from other women for an entire week? She wondered if a week without a woman was a rarity for him. Not knowing exactly what he meant by being "with another woman," she wasn't sure if she should feel offended or not.

"Well, let's go, then," she said, masking her confusion with a dazzling smile.

In a short while, they had taken their seats at one of the patio tables and ordered some drinks and a snack. The warm salty breezes managed to slip through the fences and foliage that surrounded the patio. A small number of people were seated at other tables, all casually dressed, some in damp swim suits. Their conversation was light.

Then, suddenly, he reached over to grab her hand, and she felt that he was about to say something important.

"Leah . . . tell me what it is you feel for me."

"That's what I've been trying to figure out myself," Leah confessed. "It's not an easy thing . . ."

"So you do feel something."

"Yes."

"How could I not know it," he murmured, "when I feel the way *I* do?"

Leah leaned forward. "And how do you feel?"

"The strong physical attraction is there," he said thoughtfully.

"I'll admit that." She lowered her head and smiled.

"So what do we do about it?"

Leah could not help the laughter that spilled forth. "How does a woman answer a question like that!"

Taylor ignored her laughter. "At first, I thought we could jump into the fire," he said, persuasively stroking her hand, "and give it time to burn itself out."

"We know that's not the answer," she retorted.

"I want you to know, Leah," he said softly, "that I'm willing to marry you."

Leah snorted. "That's absurd!"

"What a lovely response," said Taylor dryly.

"Well, that wasn't a very lovely proposal," she pointed out.

"Touché." He looked away. She noticed that he didn't try to rephrase the marriage "proposal," nor did she really want him to.

The sound of the breakers grew in volume as the tide rose, and the mewing of the gulls seemed to grow more piercing.

Leah withdrew her hand from Taylor's and sat, stiff and silent. She could see that he was miserable, too, in his own way. She didn't quite know what to say.

"I'm getting tired of all this sun and sand," she finally said. "It's time for me to think about leaving. I *have* gotten a lot of work done. But I'm beginning to think that this whole trip was a little bit too much of an escapist fantasy. I suppose it's impossible to escape distractions entirely. . . ." She looked up quickly to see if Taylor was insulted by her remark, but to her surprise, his expression had brightened.

"I was hoping you'd feel that way," he said.

"Why?"

"I have another proposal for you," he said, not heeding her skeptical look. "Leah, five years ago, we started an art gallery in our New York store. It was so successful that we now have galleries in some of our foreign stores. Naturally, my art buyer and I have come to know the dealers in New York very well. If you're interested in placing your work in a New York gallery, I think I could help you—not necessarily by placing your works in our gallery, though I'd like to do that sometime. I think it would be best for you if we approached a long-established dealer who deals only in art."

"You aren't joking, are you?" Leah demanded.

"I'm dead serious. Why don't you fly up with me, bring a few of your finished paintings, and we'll see what we can do?"

"You make it sound so simple!"

"It *is* simple," said Taylor easily. "My plane is here at the airport, and it can take off whenever we like." He paused. "You aren't afraid to go with me, are you?"

"Afraid? No." She studied him with her silvery blue gaze. "I suppose I'm just a little curious. Why would you want to go to so much trouble to help me like this? You aren't still trying to—"

"No!" he said roughly. "I'd really like to show you that you can trust me. And I don't think it's necessary to think I must have an ulterior motive for wanting to do this for you. It's not as though I've never done anything like this before. I've sponsored several other beginning artists whose talent I've believed in. I believe in you, Leah, and I think you deserve a chance to develop your talent. Besides—I'd love to show you New York for a few days. I'd like to show you where I live, where I work. Maybe the experience would tell you something." He was looking at her thoughtfully.

Leah touched Taylor's hand lightly with her fingers. "I think I do trust you." She laughed softly. "Just think how my mother would adore you if you were able to help me the way you think you can! She would demand to meet you and treat you like royalty."

Taylor smiled. "I'd like that. Now, what are we waiting for? You could be packing now."

"Hold on a minute. I haven't actually said I'm going."

She waited for Taylor's comeback, but there was none. He sat looking at her expectantly. The silence lengthened, broken only by the ocean sounds and the conversation of the few people remaining on the patio.

"All right, then, I'll go," she said, a bit amused at her own impetuosity.

"I'll wait right here while you pack," said Taylor quickly. "I'm ready to go myself, because I haven't unpacked yet. In fact, I didn't even bother to remove my luggage from the plane."

"So you were that sure I would go with you!" Leah exclaimed, feigning outrage. "Taylor, you're impossible! I've never met another man like you."

"Oh, no?" He raised a quizzical eyebrow. "Would you say that's because you have a rather limited circle of acquaintants?"

"No, I would *not!*" She scraped her chair back from the table and went to her room to pack.

The pilot, Taylor and Leah were the only ones aboard Taylor's private plane—along with two large,

colorful canvases and three small ones, which they
had carefully wrapped in cloths and paper found
aboard the plane. Leah was glad that she had gone
ahead with her plan to use the alkyd pigments, for
none of the oil paintings she had begun were dry
enough to be transported.

She threw occasional appreciative glances down at
the ever-changing terrain as they roared smoothly
through the skies. Taylor held her hand for much of
the trip, and they filled the hours with amiable
conversation.

"I didn't let anyone know I was leaving," confided
Leah, looking like a mischievous child. "I don't think
anyone will miss me for a few days."

"And if you stay longer than that?" asked Taylor.

"*If* I do, then I'll call my mother—and Joyce
Becker."

At last, they were circling above LaGuardia Airport, waiting to get clearance to land. It was a bumpy
landing, and Leah was grateful when she finally felt
firm ground beneath her feet.

Taylor signaled to a skycap and asked him to help
them with the paintings. They walked briskly to where
they could get a cab. Leah glanced warily about her at
the mobs of people, the noisy vehicles, the frenetically
high level of activity.

"And how is the girl from Carolina taking all this?"
he asked, grinning down at her.

"Just fine," she said. "I have been here before, you
know, if only in passing through. But it does take
getting used to, doesn't it?"

The paintings fit easily into the Checker cab. Taylor
directed the driver to a hotel on Park Avenue. He
glanced at the look on Leah's face.

"You're getting cold feet, aren't you?" he said
softly.

"I didn't know we would be staying at a hotel," she whispered. "I felt sure you had a home somewhere in New York."

"I do, but it's crawling with people right now. I didn't think you'd feel very comfortable in the midst of two sets of relatives and assorted friends of mine. That can come later. Don't worry, Leah," he said. "I reserved a suite with two bedrooms, separated by a large sitting room."

Leah thought for a moment, then began to giggle.

"What's funny?"

"I was just thinking. Most of my friends would not think twice about it if I told them I was going to stay with you in a hotel in New York. But they would find it terribly inappropriate—almost embarrassing—if they knew we planned to spend our nights in separate rooms!"

"I promise you—I won't tell anyone if you don't," he said in her ear.

Once at the hotel, they took the elevator to the third floor, then walked a distance down the hall, their footfalls noiseless in the plush carpeting. Taylor opened the door to their suite, and they entered.

"Very nice," said Leah, her comment an understatement. "It sort of makes my Ocean Inn room look—"

"I love your Florida room," he broke in.

"At least we can be sure they had different decorators."

The rooms were quintessential examples of what money and international taste could achieve. The sitting room contained several sofas and armchairs covered with raw silk, resting on a soft beige wool carpet. A giant philodendron on the low glass coffee table in the center of the room had obviously been chosen for its sculptural quality. The room was very subdued in color except for a vast abstract painting that dominated the room.

Taylor suddenly remembered the bellhop behind them whose arms were laden with Leah's paintings, and he indicated the corner where he should set them. He tipped the young man, who then left.

"Why don't you choose which bedroom you want," Taylor said to Leah, "and I'll put your suitcase in it."

Each spacious, serene bedroom had its own bathroom and large dressing room. Leah chose the one that appeared to be the more feminine of the two.

After they made a start on arranging their personal belongings, they met in the central sitting room.

"I'm very tired," announced Taylor.

"That's not surprising," said Leah. "You've done a lot of traveling today. Exactly twice as much as I have."

"Why don't we have dinner sent up tonight," he suggested, "and then turn in early." Leah listened for the subtle invitation in his voice but could detect none.

"That sounds good to me."

They ate their dinner sitting on the floor at the coffee table, then went to their respective bedrooms soon afterward. It was not long before both were sleeping soundly.

Leah was up before Taylor the next morning. But when he appeared, he sounded vigorous and full of life.

"I just called room service on the phone," he said. "We'll have breakfast; then I'd like to take you shopping."

"Shopping, fine! But not at just any store, I hope," she teased.

"I only know of one department store in New York," Taylor replied, a mischievous glint in his eye. "You mean to tell me there are others?"

An hour later, they were on the gray turbulent streets of New York, looking for a cab. When they finally found one, Taylor directed the driver to an address on Fifth Avenue.

Leah could see the gigantic script from a distance. It was several stories up the side of the monumental building, and it read: CAMBRIDGE PAYNE.

"It looks stupendous from here," said Leah.

"The only real problem we're having now is parking," Taylor told her. "The parking garage is almost always full, so we're in the process of making some additions to it. It goes down many more levels than it appears to from the outside."

"It sounds like quite an undertaking."

The cab let them off right in front of the store, and they walked through the gleaming revolving doors that fronted the street. Once inside, Leah realized she was in the presence of the highest concentration of tasteful and outrageously expensive merchandise that she had ever seen. Crystal decanters of rich perfumes sparkled on the counter tops. To the right were designer scarves and handbags in gorgeous colors, silk and leather; to the left was row upon row of jewelry displays, softly shining gold and silver, diamonds in fabulous settings. And this was just the beginning, as Leah was soon to find out.

As they moved through the store, Leah noticed that some of the salesclerks reacted visibly when they recognized Taylor. He seemed to leave behind him a wake of whispers and increased activity.

They passed through the makeup department where elegantly dressed women were seated in front of mirrors while consultants applied the latest shades of makeup to their faces. Then they glided up a long escalator to the second floor.

"I want to introduce you to a friend of mine," said Taylor.

Occupying half of the second floor was a large art gallery. The works, mostly contemporary, were displayed to perfection on smooth gray walls.

Taylor was pleased to see Leah's look of interest. "I hope you approve," he said.

"It's wonderful!"

"Come on. I want you to meet my art buyer."

He led her to the back of the gallery. He found the woman he was looking for and introduced her as Polly Rutherford.

". . . and Polly, I'd like you to meet Leah Du-Chaine."

"It's a pleasure." The two women shook hands.

Polly Rutherford was tall and very thin and looked as if she were in her late thirties. She wore a narrow-skirted red suit, and her dark hair was short and chic. She looked at Leah out of dark appraising eyes. Leah was uncomfortably aware that for some reason this woman did not like her.

"I suppose you are one of Taylor's new artists?" said Polly in her cool, dry voice.

"I'm not sure exactly how to answer that question," said Leah with composure, "but yes, I am an artist."

"And you would like to be represented in our gallery?" Her manner seemed not to admit of the possibility that Leah could be there for any other reason.

Leah opened her mouth to speak, but Taylor spoke quickly.

"Polly, Leah's a friend of mine," he said. "I brought her here because I thought she'd be interested in seeing the store. I hope she will eventually place some paintings in our gallery, but we have other plans for her right now. Plans I think you can help us with." He gave her a wink.

"Sounds interesting," said Polly noncommittally.

Then she turned to Taylor and engaged him in a lengthy discussion that necessarily excluded Leah since it was concerned with store business. Leah could tell by watching them together that Taylor and Polly had a very close working relationship. She could also sense that Polly considered her, Leah, an interloper.

The two women exchanged pleasantries when Polly's discussion with Taylor was over. Taylor and Leah turned to leave, and when they were a safe distance away, Leah spoke in Taylor's ear.

"That woman didn't like me *at all,*" she whispered.

Taylor did not believe her. "That's ridiculous. Polly's an old friend. She wouldn't judge you on such short acquaintance." Leah saw that he was leading her toward the dress department. "Come on. I want you to try some dresses on for me."

"Taylor." Leah gave him a level look. "Please don't put me in this position. You know how I feel about that."

"Please, it's purely a business interest. I'd really like to see what a store like ours would come up with if a woman as beautiful as you are walked in and asked to see some dresses. Don't tell me you wouldn't enjoy trying on some of our designer clothes."

"Why do I have the feeling that no matter what I say, you're going to talk me into it?" said Leah with a sigh.

"Good girl!" He squeezed her arm.

A pleasant young redhead waited on them, bringing out armfuls of exclusive designer creations, some feminine and frothy, some exquisitely fashioned with thousands of tiny beads sewn on by hand, some stunning in their intelligent simplicity and perfect cut.

Leah tried many of them on, daring evening gowns to simple afternoon dresses, modeling them all for Taylor till she was dizzy. To her surprise, he had been right. She did enjoy it. She felt like another woman entirely as she pirouetted before the mirrors in dresses so fabulous that she felt they should have existed only in dreams.

Taylor liked the simple ones on her best, especially those in the more vivid colors.

When the modeling session was over, Leah was exhausted. Taylor indicated they would take the elevator, and the two of them started off for it.

Then Taylor fell back to whisper something to the young salesclerk.

Leah turned to see what he was doing. She stood stock-still, her face set in irritation. Quickly, she walked back to where Taylor and the salesclerk stood talking. She was just in time to hear him whisper, "Wrap them up and send them to my hotel."

"No!" protested Leah, ignoring the startled look on the salesgirl's face.

"Darling, don't deny me the pleasure of buying you some new clothes," Taylor said softly and urgently.

Leah was suddenly aware that she would cause him great embarrassment by refusing his gift in front of his employee. She didn't want him to lose face, but she was determined not to compromise her principles. How could she countermand his request without making a scene?

Taylor coaxed, "Darling, I want to take you to a special place for dinner, and—"

"My white silk will do just fine, don't you think?" Leah inquired sweetly.

"You know I love it, but you looked so wonderful in the blue one."

The salesgirl had retreated a few steps and was doing her best to appear as if she didn't hear a word they were saying. Leah thought quickly.

"Well . . . maybe you're right, darling," she said with an emphasis on the word "darling" so slight that she knew only Taylor would detect it. "Maybe I *should* take the blue one." Fortunately, she had noticed that the blue dress was inexpensive in comparison with the other creations, though the price was still enough to take her breath away. She considered a moment, then said, "Yes." She turned to the clerk. "Please wrap that one up."

"And send it to the hotel," growled Taylor. He stalked off in the direction of the elevator.

Leah caught up with him and whispered loudly in his ear. "I'll write you a check when we get back to the hotel!" she hissed.

Taylor's face darkened. "It will be a cold day in hell—" he began.

"All right, I'll pay you the wholesale cost, not the retail, if that will make you feel better."

"We'll discuss it later." Taylor gave the elevator button a savage poke. "Let's have lunch. At the hotel."

Forty-five minutes later, they were seated in the sumptuous dining room on the main floor of the hotel. They occupied themselves with discussing the menu; then Taylor ordered quiche for Leah and a small filet for himself. They sat in silence for a few minutes.

"You were going to get me more than one dress, weren't you?" asked Leah, her voice faintly accusing.

Taylor looked at her, a hard light in his eyes. "Yes, I was," he said. "I was going to get you the red lace dress . . . and the long green one . . . and that other blue one. Teal blue, I think they call it. It would have looked good with your hair. I was sure that once you opened them up . . . in the hotel room . . . you would be so happy with them that you would forget those silly principles of yours."

Leah stared at him in disbelief. "Maybe that's how you get your other women," she said in a condemning whisper, "but those techniques don't work with me."

"I didn't mean I planned on persuading you to forget *all* your principles!" said Taylor with exasperation. "I'm not as calculating as all that!"

The waiter arrived with the food, and sedately they began to eat.

"I think I know what the problem is," said Leah finally. "We come from such different worlds. I don't think you can understand the way I look at things—"

"I understand that people in your world don't seem very gracious about accepting gifts!"

Leah took a deep breath, keeping her temper in check. "Taylor," she said patiently, "women like me do not accept gifts worth thousands of dollars from men that they've known for a week and a half! Call it provincial if you will." She paused. "Maybe it was a big mistake for me to come to New York with you. I probably shouldn't have agreed to let you help me with my career—much as I appreciate the idea. I really don't think I can change the way I am—and I'm not sure that I want to."

Taylor stopped eating for a moment and looked at her wordlessly. Then, all at once, she could see a smile deep in his eyes. When he spoke, his voice was gentle for the first time since they had left Cambridge Payne. "I don't think I want you to change," he said. "And please, let's not break up our business relationship—or our personal one."

Leah continued her meal in puzzled silence. She had felt herself to be in the middle of an unsolvable conflict with the man seated across from her; a battle of wills in which no one could be the winner. Then, suddenly, she had seen that she had pleased him somehow. It wasn't important enough to be called a victory. But where there had been tension between them, Taylor's smiling eyes and voice evoked peace.

"Leah, you know you can't afford that dress," said Taylor reasonably.

"You forget I just made a big sale. I can afford it."

"But it costs me nothing—"

"Maybe not directly—"

"What about your financial security? I know you need it in order to paint."

Leah laughed. "I'm counting on you to help me make a big splash in New York! Which brings up another subject—"

"Why do I have the feeling I'm not going to like this very much?" he asked, looking up at the ceiling.

"If I do sell any paintings, I hope you are planning to take a percentage of the sales as my agent."

Taylor took one of her hands in his, leaned forward and spoke as one does when humoring a small child. "Leah, I'll do whatever makes you happy," he said.

Leah grimaced, but she finished her meal in a fairly good humor.

They did a little sightseeing that afternoon, then returned to the hotel to prepare for dinner. Leah stepped out of her room wearing the new blue dress. The color was deep and beautiful, the material soft and clingy, and it had a draped neckline that was subtly provocative. She was shyly aware of her own beauty. Her hair was worn loose about her shoulders.

"Look," she said, "you've finally convinced me to wear my hair down."

"You look gorgeous," he said.

"Is this better than the baggy jeans and T-shirts?" She turned around slowly, the hem of the dress swishing softly about her knees.

"Mm, much." He looked at her, considering. He went to her, took her firmly by the shoulders and kissed her on the forehead.

Given what she had seen of Taylor's life-style, Leah had expected that he would take her to a famous New York restaurant such as the Four Seasons or the 21 Club. But he took her to an unprepossessing establishment on East Fifty-second Street that didn't even have a sign out front.

The maître d' greeted Taylor by name and led the couple through the front room to a smaller room at the back. It was an intimate room, almost masculine, with its darkly paneled walls and faint traces of cigar smoke. It glimmered with candlelight and highly polished silver. Taylor told Leah that the restaurant was blessed with one of the finest chefs in the city.

"I will direct your friends to your table when they arrive, sir," said the maître d', and he left.

Leah looked at Taylor. "So we won't be dining alone?" she asked.

"One of my reasons for bringing you to the city was to introduce you to some of my friends," he explained. "You don't mind, do you?"

"Of course not."

But when Polly Rutherford appeared in the doorway, Leah had a feeling of foreboding. Polly was with a short balding man who turned out to have some importance in the field of publishing. One other couple then joined them, a young Broadway actress and her boy friend, who was a producer.

Taylor's friends were an articulate and gregarious group, and Leah sat quietly, infrequently offering a comment. She watched Taylor, fascinated with the sophistication and air of control that became even more obvious when he was with these people. She was also intrigued by Polly, who was very clever and even scathing when she was addressing comments to anyone at the table except Taylor. When she looked at him, her voice and her eyes softened.

I was right, thought Leah to herself. *She does have a thing for Taylor.*

Leah and Taylor left the group early, and she sat close to him in the taxi on the way to the hotel.

"I was proud of you," said Taylor matter-of-factly.

"You were?" asked Leah in surprise. "I certainly didn't hold my own in the conversation."

"Oh, but you did," he corrected. "You were quieter than the others, but there's an aura about you that they don't have . . . a strength, a beauty."

She chuckled deprecatingly and nestled closer to him.

"You didn't hate it, did you?" he asked with concern.

"Oh, no! It was very enjoyable. Except, perhaps, for Polly's evil eye."

Taylor shrugged off her comment. "I think you're wrong about her."

For a few moments, he seemed lost in thought. Then he took a breath. "Sometimes I get tired of my way of life," he said. "I am very attracted to, even envious of, your way of life: the creative solitude, the singleness of purpose."

"Is that why you're attracted to me?" she asked with curiosity.

"It's one of the things I like about you." He smiled, bent to kiss her deeply on the mouth, then broke away to smile at her again. "You *know* things won't get out of hand while we're still in here," he said.

She offered her lips to him again, enjoying the sensations that coursed through her body as they kissed passionately in the dark back seat of the moving taxi.

Once inside the suite, they sat in the sitting room for an hour, Leah on the couch, Taylor on a chair facing her. Leah lost herself in the rhythm of their conversation. Their talk was free and intense, each seeming to want to search out the thoughts and feelings of the other. At last, Taylor stood up abruptly and told her he was going to bed. He walked off to his room.

Leah switched off the lights and went to her own room.

She removed her elegant dress and put on her night shift. Once in bed, she lay awake, sorrowful and confused. She was honest enough to admit to herself that she felt a powerful physical longing for Taylor and that she was puzzled by his behavior. What a confusing man he was. He had come on so strong when she first met him, even saying that he did not trust himself to be alone with her. But now that she was spending the night in the same hotel suite with him, he seemed able to hold himself at a distance without much apparent effort.

She rumpled the sheets as she twisted uneasily in her bed, her fever of longing no less real than a fever due to illness.

Chapter Seven

When Leah awoke the next morning, the sun was filtering through the thin metal blinds that hung in her room. She washed her face, dressed quickly in her skirt and blouse, then stroked on a bit of gray eye shadow in the creases of her lids and a touch of rose-colored blush on her cheekbones. She brushed her hair vigorously till it shone with a luminous blondeness. Ruefully, she glanced down at her outfit. She would have to buy some new clothes, if only another blouse or two to go with her skirt, if she remained much longer in New York.

When she came out into the sitting room, she saw Taylor seated in a corner of the sofa, reading the *Times*. He looked up, and his face brightened at the sight of her.

But something seemed a little artificial to her about the whole situation. She sank back onto the sofa with a dejected air. "I'm really not filling my role very well," she said. "I guess I hadn't thought ahead far enough to what would be expected of me."

"What are you talking about?" Taylor set his newspaper down on the table, keeping his eyes on her face.

"Well, what's generally expected of a woman when a man flies her to another city—when he pays for her hotel, her meals, and at least tries to lavish extravagant clothing on her?" She rubbed the beige silk of the sofa with her fingers.

"I haven't put any pressure on you at all, have I?" he said softly. "Don't you understand what that means?"

"What does it mean?"

"That I'm trying to show you something. That I'm willing to abide by your wishes. I want you to see I'm not such a rogue as you think."

Leah smiled, but she wondered if this was just another way to get to her. Was it all an act to gain her favor?

Taylor must have sensed the kind of thought that was going through her head; when she looked at him, she saw that his dark eyes were disturbed. "If you'd like, we could fly back right now, this afternoon."

"But you'd like me to stay a little longer?"

"Of course I would. Today is the day we take steps to launch your career. Look." He pointed to the empty corner where her canvases had been stacked till now. "I've already sent your paintings to our gallery, where we can keep them till they find their new home."

Leah had a strong impulse to go to him and throw her arms around his neck. But she just said in a sincere voice, "I would be glad to stay a while longer."

"Then it's settled. Come on. Let's go downstairs for

breakfast. Then we'll call Polly and talk to her about showing your paintings around."

They converged on the door that opened into the hall. Taylor reached for Leah's arm, grasped it firmly and turned her to look at him. He looked deeply into her blue eyes.

"I'm trying, Leah," he said enigmatically. "Just give me a little more time."

"Time for what?" she asked in surprise.

But he just shook his head and lightly propelled her through the door.

"I'll try not to be too dictatorial while we launch your career," he said as they walked down the hall. "It's a habit of mine—one I'll try to break where you're concerned. But I know a lot of dealers in the city, and it won't hurt you to approach them through already-established channels. With Polly doing the leg work—" Leah glanced away, and Taylor looked at her with perplexity. "Come on, now. Why so glum? Polly always handles this side of the business for me, and she's damn good at it. Regardless of your feelings about her, I believe she's the best person for the job."

"Do you think she'll want to?" she asked doubtfully.

"Of course! She's a good friend of mine, and I just can't believe she dislikes you as much as you think she does."

They took the elevator downstairs, entered the dining room and ordered breakfast. While they were waiting for the food to arrive, Taylor went to call Polly. During his brief absence, Leah's mind touched on the implications of Taylor's generous offer to help her career. Was it an attempt to bind her more closely to him by making her feel obligated to him?

When Taylor returned, he told her that Polly had

agreed to meet them for lunch at a Chinese restaurant on Third Avenue.

After breakfast, Leah and Taylor spent the morning in Central Park, strolling through the tract of rural splendor that was ringed by skyscrapers. The sun was pleasantly hot, the scenery was beautiful, and since school was out for the summer, there were many children laughing and playing.

At quarter to twelve, they left the park and took a taxi to the restaurant where Polly was already waiting. Her hair was carefully coiffed, and she had applied her eye makeup with a heavy touch. Her couture suit was the latest fashion; a single lapel was snow white, and the rest of the outfit was a brilliant emerald green. She is attractive, thought Leah, giving her a narrow look. I suppose it would depend on a man's taste. And whether or not he liked older women.

Polly gave Taylor an affectionate peck on the cheek, then shook Leah's hand civilly. The three were led into the main dining area. It was the most sumptuous Chinese restaurant that Leah had ever seen, with cascades of fresh flowers and fine paintings on the walls. All three ordered a special dish of shrimp, meat, bamboo shoots and vegetables wrapped in a Chinese pancake.

"Polly!" began Taylor with enthusiasm after an appropriate amount of small talk. "You and I are about to embark on a special project: launching the career of Leah DuChaine!"

Leah hid a smile at the expression on Polly's face, which was less than enthusiastic.

"That sounds marvelous," said Polly. "How do I fit in?" Daintily, she picked up a morsel of shrimp with her chopsticks—she and Taylor both ate skillfully with chopsticks.

Taylor said he had had Leah's paintings delivered to the gallery that morning.

"Yes, they did arrive," said Polly cautiously, as if she weren't quite sure what they were doing there.

Taylor asked her if she would show them about town, take them to the galleries she thought best.

"Of course, I'd be delighted to," said Polly. Her glance flickered across the table to Leah. "You're a very lucky young lady," she said, "to have Taylor Cambridge willing to help your career this way. Most artists are forced to struggle a bit more to get established."

"I know, and I'm grateful," said Leah, trying to inject a note of humility into her voice because Polly seemed to expect it.

"Ah, Polly," said Taylor, touching her hand, "if Leah didn't have me to help her, it would just take her a bit longer, that's all. Because she has true talent."

"I know that." And Polly turned to Taylor and flashed him a smile.

How cold she is to me and how amiable with Taylor, thought Leah.

"Polly, you know I value your opinion," said Taylor. "No one knows the market better than you do. Where do you think would be the best place to start?"

"With Jacques Léon," said Polly, glowing at Taylor's praise of her expertise.

"And why is that?"

"Because he's the best," she replied crisply. "Leah, you'd like to have a chance with the best, wouldn't you?"

Leah nodded, feeling a little ashamed. Perhaps she had been wrong about Polly. Perhaps the woman was actually quite willing to help her without complaining.

One certainly couldn't blame her for being enamored of Taylor; Leah herself was painfully aware that it was only too easy to respond to his magnetism and dark good looks. She couldn't even blame Polly for her apparent jealousy of herself. She decided to give Polly the benefit of the doubt.

So it was determined that Polly would call Jacques Léon, the famous gallery owner, that afternoon and set up a time to show him Leah's paintings. As Leah listened to the details of the project being discussed, the whole thing became more and more real to her, and with a jolt she realized that being represented in a New York gallery would put many of her dreams within the realm of possibility.

"I really am fortunate to have the two of you to help me," she said, and this time the note of thankfulness in her voice was real.

"Leave everything to us, my dear," said Polly, touching her lightly on the shoulder. "With Taylor and me on your side, your success is assured."

After lunch, Taylor told Leah apologetically that it was time he got some work done. He asked her if she wished to go to a matinee, go back to the hotel or if there was something else she'd rather do. She opted for spending a few hours at the Metropolitan Museum.

The three of them climbed into a cab, which made its way through the traffic, at last depositing Leah in front of the Metropolitan. She started up the grand sweep of steps, and the taxi containing Polly and Taylor pulled away from the curb.

After several hours of roaming the galleries of the museum, Leah took a taxi back to the hotel, where she was to meet Taylor. He was not back yet, so she looked at some magazines and wandered restlessly about the suite. Her heart lifted when she heard his key in the door.

"Taylor!" There was perhaps a trace too much gladness in her voice as Taylor walked through the door, she thought. After all, they had merely spent an afternoon apart.

"Are you that happy to see me?" he asked with a smile. "I'm sorry I abandoned you this afternoon," he said. "I'll make it up to you this evening. I have a very special place in mind for dinner.

"Do you ever go to any other kind of place?" she teased.

Taylor folded his arms around her and gave her a sweet, closed-mouth kiss.

"You look very pretty," he said.

"I feel like a hag. I guess I'm just not used to the city pace."

Taylor leaned back to regard her, his hands still on her waist. "Maybe you'd rather we eat in tonight," he suggested. "We can lock out all the other people we've known and all our worries about the future and all the people currently in our lives who might be trying to get to us. No one can find us—no one knows where we are."

"That sounds like heaven."

Taylor called room service and ordered steak au poivre, and a good bottle of Cabernet. Leah stood motionless in front of the window, gazing at the city spread out below her, at the shining lights that were starting to wink on as darkness descended.

She felt Taylor approach her from behind after he hung up the phone, felt his warm breath on her neck just before he began to nuzzle her. His hands fell lightly on her shoulders.

"How about a back rub before dinner?" he offered.

She gladly accepted and went to the couch to stretch out on it, face down. Taylor sat beside her and began to knead firmly the tight muscles of her back and neck, forcing the tension out as Leah groaned in appreciation.

"You have magic hands, my friend," she said.

"Mm-hm," he agreed.

Taylor's hands began to make forays over different parts of Leah's body. He worked lower and lower down her spine till he came to the soft roundness of her hips. Then he turned her slightly to one side and gradually worked his fingers over her back, across her side and then to the front so that he was just barely caressing her breasts.

"Is that part of the standard back rub?" asked Leah.

"I can't help it," said Taylor with mock chagrin.

There came a sharp knock at the door. "Room service," said Taylor regretfully. Leah sat up and combed her hair with her fingers as Taylor went to open the door.

"Room service, sir."

"Will you please wheel it right there in front of the couch?"

The dark-haired little man complied, accepted his tip and left.

"What a feast," said Leah with admiration as they sat down to the gourmet dinner. "Such a heavenly aroma." She savored the wine, which was light and flavorful. "Funny thing about wine. With the first sip I take, I feel warm right down to my toes."

"Are you warm now?" Taylor arched his eyebrows at her.

"Yes," she said, and they shared a wine-flavored kiss.

By now Leah's fatigue had given way to feelings of blissful serenity. The room seemed to be filled with pleasure and love, and to Leah it seemed right that all others were excluded. This evening was hers and Taylor's alone to share, just as he had promised.

That was why it was such a shock when the phone began to ring. "Who could that be?" exclaimed Taylor, his startled look matching Leah's. He strode over to the phone in the corner of the room. Leah's heart constricted with apprehension. Surely it must be terrible news if someone could track them down to their hideaway when Taylor and she had made sure that no one knew where they were.

But her unease turned to anger when she heard the name "Polly" on Taylor's lips as he spoke into the receiver. Polly Rutherford! How did *Polly* know where she and Taylor were staying? Leah felt that her privacy had been unpleasantly invaded. Why had Taylor given Polly his number?

Leah's anger grew in proportion to the length of time Taylor continued to speak on the phone. She wondered why he didn't tell Polly he was busy and bring the conversation to a close. He kept his back toward Leah as he spoke, and she made no attempt to overhear what he was saying. She really didn't want to know.

At last, Taylor replaced the receiver in its cradle, and he turned around to face Leah's flashing blue eyes. "I thought you said no one knew where we were," she said.

"Leah," said Taylor, taking a few steps toward her, "even when I'm keeping a low profile, I always have to let two people know where they can reach me in case of an emergency: Jack Struan, my right-hand man, and . . . Polly. She's been with me a long time and has a unique position in the company. I'm responsible for a major corporation, and if something were to go wrong—"

"Did she know I was here?" interrupted Leah.

"I don't know. I doubt it."

Leah wondered how Polly could possibly not know. She and Taylor had been discreet when they conversed before Polly, but Leah felt sure that Polly would have concluded that she was staying with Taylor even if she had *not* been staying with him. Leah imagined that Polly felt jealous and powerless to do anything about the situation. Her phone call, she was sure, was a pathetic attempt to make some kind of contact with Taylor and perhaps to stir up a little trouble.

"So they're to call you only in case of emergency," repeated Leah.

"Yes, they're under strict instructions to call me only if a problem can be handled only by me and cannot wait."

"And did Polly's problem fall into that category?"

Taylor's rugged features took on a trace of uncertainty. "Actually, it was a very minor problem," he admitted. "I can't think why she bothered me about it."

"Well, maybe you'll believe me now when I tell you she's in love with you—and she's jealous of me!" There was a note of triumph in Leah's voice now that she thought Taylor would be forced to admit the obvious.

"You little witch," said Taylor amiably. "This is a side of you I've never seen before." He continued walking toward her.

Leah's eyes widened. "There's probably a lot about me that you don't know."

Taylor laid his hands on her shoulders and looked at

her steadily. "Leah," he said, "there's no need for *you* to be jealous, you know. Even if what you say about Polly is true, I feel nothing more for her than friendship."

Leah forced a laugh. *"I'm* not jealous!" she insisted. "I was only upset because you refused to admit the truth about Polly. And I got upset when the phone rang because you told me no one knew where we were, and then when it was *she—"*

"I understand," said Taylor.

His voice was calming, but there was still a frown between Leah's eyes. "It must be awfully difficult for her to try to peddle my paintings, feeling the way she does."

"I don't think so—she's a professional. I think you underestimate her, Leah."

She pulled away from his grasp and turned toward the table. "We might as well finish our dinner," she said.

They enjoyed the rest of the dinner, but the special mood of the evening had been lost—so much so that Leah had an attack of conscience when she was through eating and decided she must immediately notify her mother and Joyce Becker of her whereabouts.

She telephoned the Ocean Inn first and was glad when it was Joyce who answered the phone.

"Leah!" exclaimed Joyce. "Where in the world are you?"

"New York City. I'm here with a friend."

"Thank goodness! Rhoda Hughes called yesterday —right after we began to worry about your absence. She said that she had an idea where you had gone and that we shouldn't call the police yet."

"The police! You mean you thought something had happened to me?" Perhaps they had thought she had been kidnaped. "My mother didn't call, did she?" she asked apprehensively.

"I don't believe so; there are no messages for you. Please understand, we don't like to intrude in our guests' private lives, but when no one had seen you for a day and a half, yet your car was still here—"

"I do understand," said Leah, grateful that her sudden disappearance hadn't caused more of an uproar.

"So you're all right? You're not—"

"I'm not being held hostage," Leah said, laughing. "And now I think I should call my mother!"

Leah did not try to explain everything when she reached her mother on the line. She merely told her that she was in New York, that it was something to do with her career and that she hoped to have some good news for her soon. Her mother was a little bewildered, but she reacted with equanimity. She did admonish her to be careful.

After she hung up the phone, she turned to see Taylor watching her, a half smile on his face. He had turned on some soft music while she was talking to her mother, and he held the wine bottle and her empty glass in his hands. "Have some more wine?" he offered.

"I'd love to." She stood just looking at him for a moment as he filled her glass. He looked so good to her, everything about him—the way he moved, his intelligent eyes and heart-stopping smile, the calm, courteous manner that could not hide the male dynamism beneath. She accepted the wine, and they sat and talked for a while. She felt herself being more drawn to him than ever before.

This time, it was Leah who suddenly stood and said it was time she turned in for the night.

Chapter Eight

When Leah came out of her room the following morning, Taylor was waiting for her in the sitting room, dressed in a light gray suit, sun-lightened hair casually combed and still damp from his shower. He gave her an engaging grin. He had already ordered a breakfast from room service, and it was spread out before him on the coffee table: succulent fresh fruit, crusty buttered bread and hot coffee.

Leah was so hungry that she ate without pausing to speak. Finally sated, she sat back with a sigh. She looked at Taylor from beneath her dark lashes. Sunlight was streaming through the cantilevered blinds. A sharp awareness of her own feelings had come upon her suddenly, and she was almost astonished when she realized what they were. Something had been happening to her over the last few days, so gradually that she hadn't really noticed till now. The almost automatic irritation that she had initially felt with Taylor had vanished, and behind the screen of her negative feelings she discovered another emotion. Though not daring yet to give it a name, she recognized that her physical attraction to Taylor was being transformed into something much deeper.

"I can't stop smiling," she said. "I feel very happy this morning."

"It's wonderful what a good breakfast can do," murmured Taylor. He grasped her hand and pulled her to her feet. "Are you ready to leave? I have some place special I want to take you."

They took the elevator down to the lobby, then walked through the revolving doors out onto the hot city streets. The air was muggy, the sidewalks were crowded, and the streets were filled with the sounds of idling engines and the impatient blasts of horns. Taylor hailed a taxi, and he and Leah slid into the passenger seat of a stately Checker cab.

The cab took them around Central Park to 88th Street where it deposited them in front of the six-story spiral that was the Guggenheim Museum.

"You've never been inside before, have you?" asked Taylor, and Leah said that she had not. With deep appreciation, her eyes traveled over the marvelous building about which she had heard so much.

They took the elevator to the top of the spiral, got out and then began their slow circular descent around the uniquely designed interior. The walls were lined with paintings and drawings, all contemporary, and there was also whimsical sculpture that sometimes bordered on the bizarre.

Taylor pointed to a stack of nine large weathered pieces of wood that formed a large cube on the floor. "Leah, you understand all this better than I do," he said. "That's obviously meant to be a work of art. See, there's the little card that gives it a title—or does it say 'Untitled'?" He moved in closer. "Leah, I sincerely wish you'd explain it to me."

"The artist probably appreciated the rough texture of the wood and thought it would be interesting to put it in a symmetrical arrangement. Maybe he thought most people wouldn't notice the beauty in plain old pieces of weathered wood unless he stacked them up and put them on public display." She smiled a secret smile and glanced about to see if anyone else was listening. "If you want my honest opinion, I think there's so much more you can do with a work of art."

She almost laughed at Taylor's look of relief. "Do you mean to tell me there's not some subtle philosophy in this piece that I'm too uneducated to understand?"

"I have my own opinions about that," answered Leah. "I'm not saying this work doesn't have a thing to say. But I think it's possible to say the same thing, or more, in a work that is also beautiful, complex or skillfully made. Look at that metal sculpture over there."

There were many works in the museum that both agreed were superb. Leah was delighted to find that she could view a work from a short distance, then make a half turn around the spiral and look back across the vast inner space of the building to view the same work from a great distance.

At last, Taylor glanced at his watch. "It's getting close to lunch time," he said. "Let's grab another cab and have lunch at Alexandra's."

"That sounds good. I'm famished again."

"Urban living seems to have stimulated your appetite!"

Leah sat close to Taylor in the taxi, close enough to be aware of his warmth and the faint spicy scent of his cologne. When he smiled down at her, his warm brown eyes crinkling at the edges, it was as if they shared a special secret. His closeness, his touch, warmed her with a kind of promise.

Once at Alexandra's, Taylor ordered chicken in wine sauce for both of them—and it was delicious.

Leah was fascinated by the many beautiful women dining in the restaurant. Some of them were quite elegant; some were dressed in fashionable clothing that was fanciful, even humorous. Taylor noticed what she was looking at.

"I prefer the beauty that's sitting at my table," he said, smiling.

"Tell me, Taylor," she said suddenly. "Just why did you bring me to New York? Oh, I know all the obvious reasons, but it seems there's something more—"

"You're very perceptive," he said, taking her hand. "I think you've probably guessed that I am . . . serious about you."

Leah said nothing. "Serious" was a rather ambiguous word, and she wasn't sure what he meant by it.

For the first time since she had known this handsome, strong man, he seemed to be faltering. "I wanted to show you my world," he said. "I wanted to get your reaction to it. If you find it totally repugnant —well, that would say something about any future we might have together, wouldn't it?"

A kind of warning signal had sounded inside of Leah. So he thought they might have a future together. And he seemed to be saying that he wanted to bring her into *his* way of life. She thought of her sister Eve and how her husband had very gently, very undemandingly, drawn her into his own way of life— to the exclusion of her own dreams. No, she wouldn't let that happen to her no matter how she felt about Taylor.

"No, of course I don't find it repugnant," she said. "I've enjoyed myself greatly. But I do think there's quite a difference in our priorities, don't you?"

"I think you've taught me something about priorities," said Taylor, his voice husky with emotion. Leah wondered if it could be true. If Taylor were willing to accommodate himself to her way of life, then she was in danger, for in the last few days she had found herself falling deeper and deeper into something like love—a deep appreciation of Taylor, sensual pleasure at his nearness, a delightful heart skipping when he appeared after a short absence. And yet another thought was nagging at Leah, the thought that she should be getting back to Vero Beach, back to her work.

Taylor glanced at his watch. "I think I'll call the hotel," he said. "I want to see if there are any messages for me." Leah looked up at him in surprise, wondering why he suddenly felt he had to catch up on his messages just when they seemed to be discovering something important in their relationship. He caught her look and leaned over to chide her before he stood. "I don't mean just any messages," he said. "I want to see if Polly's had a chance to get somebody to look at your work."

When he reappeared, he asked Leah if she were ready to leave. "She left a message an hour ago," he said. "She wants me to meet her at the gallery."

"I hope it's good news," said Leah, her voice a bit more fervent than she liked.

Taylor gave her shoulders an encouraging squeeze.

He and Leah began walking in the direction of Fifth Avenue till they were able to catch a taxi that took them the rest of the way to the store. When they reached the top of the escalator at the second floor, they could see into the gallery. It was empty of browsers, but they could see the tall, thin form of Polly in a far corner.

She came forward to greet them as they walked into the gallery. Leah could tell that she had some significant news for them, and she tried to read the art buyer's face, but it was devoid of expression.

"I have something to show you," said Polly, turning on her heel, and they followed her to a room behind the gallery where her desk and files were kept. She picked up an envelope from the top of the desk and placed it in Taylor's hands.

Leah watched Taylor remove a folded piece of paper from the envelope and saw his face darken as he quickly scanned its contents. Silently, he began to stuff it back into the envelope, but Leah calmly reached for it.

"Please," she begged, "I have to see what he said."

Above Jacques Léon's elaborate signature was a short hand-written note. Leah's stomach tightened as she read his comments on her work.

We decline the opportunity to exhibit the work by the artist Leah DuChaine. We find the paintings too conventional in conception and amateurish in technique to meet our standards. We suggest the artist try a market other than New York.

Jacques Léon

"Honey—" began Taylor.

"Oh, I'm not upset," said Leah hastily. "Puzzled, perhaps. Of course, it's his right not to accept my work, but—conventional? Amateurish? No one's ever called me that before!"

"He obviously doesn't know what he's talking about!" said Taylor with scorn.

"Jacques Léon is a tough critic," said Polly, very unhelpfully, Leah thought.

"Maybe he's right about one thing," said Leah. "I might be out of my league in New York."

"No!" Taylor contradicted her. "We'll just try again. We'll find a dealer with better taste—and one a bit more polite! Polly, I'd like you to show the paintings to George Mayer."

"As you wish," said Polly with a thin smile.

Taylor took Leah's arm and turned abruptly to leave. As they came to the outer limit of the gallery, Leah glanced back at Polly. She was standing in the doorway to the back room, looking after Taylor's and Leah's retreating backs, the smile still on her face.

They dined at Lutèce that night. Its exquisite cuisine rivaled the finest Leah had sampled during her stay in Europe. They lingered over the five-course meal, but there was still time for a visit to Taylor's favorite night club where a pianist masterfully played classics from Broadway shows and some jazz.

It was early morning before they made it back to the hotel. Once inside the room, Taylor gathered Leah into his arms. She could tell, as always, that there was something restrained in the way he held her. She felt her own body, almost involuntarily, go soft and melting against him.

"Don't do that!" said Taylor, and she was surprised to hear real anger in his voice.

"I was just hugging you back," she reproached him. "I was just feeling all warm and happy and—"

"Leah," he said sternly, holding her at arm's length, "sometimes I think you're doing your best to push me to the limits of my self-control. Don't you know there's only so much a man can stand!"

Leah was looking down at the floor. "Do you mean I can't touch you or hug you if I feel like it?"

"Just don't start anything you're not willing to finish," he said quietly.

Leah pulled softly away from his grasp and stood facing him from several feet away. They hadn't bothered to turn on the lights when they came into the room, but the blinds were pulled up to the top of the window, revealing the panorama of the city, with its thousands of lights. The sky was not as inky black as it had been an hour earlier; a barely perceptible lightening in the east said that it would soon be dawn.

"I'm sorry if I make things difficult for you," she said in a small voice.

"Don't worry about it." Taylor shoved his hands in his pockets and walked over to the window.

Leah remained still in the same spot. "Taylor, I'd like to ask you something. Not that I'm anxious to change the subject—"

"Oh, yes, you are!" he said with a short laugh.

"—but do you think Polly is as glad to help me as she makes out?"

"Of course she is," he said, stalking over to the sofa and sitting back on it.

Leah followed him with her eyes. "And you still don't think she's jealous of me—because she's in love with you?"

"I'm sure she's fond of me, but that's as far as it goes." He tried to hide a yawn.

Leah walked to the other end of the sofa and sat, smoothing her dress over her knees. "But I'd like to know something—unless you think I have no right to ask. Was there ever anything between you and Polly? I mean, did you ever reciprocate—?"

"You intend to pursue this subject to the bitter end, don't you!" Taylor sounded weary. "But I don't mind telling you that, yes, Polly and I did have a brief fling. But that was seventeen years ago. I was in college at the time, and my father had set me to work in the store between school sessions. That was when I met her. She was working at Cambridge Payne even then."

"Isn't she quite a bit older than you?" asked Leah.

"Leah," said Taylor patiently, "there's a greater distance between your age and mine than there is between hers and mine! Do you think I'm too old for *you?*"

"I suppose not."

Taylor went on reflectively. "She was young at the time, but she *was* older and more experienced than I was. She took a liking to me. She coached me in how to handle my father. He and I did have some run-ins at the time! In some ways, she was my mentor, you might say."

"In the bedroom as well as in business." Leah's tone was reserved.

Taylor sat forward suddenly. "Leah, I'm not going to get defensive about this. I was very young, eighteen years old, and that was a long time ago. Perhaps she took advantage of me"—he ignored Leah's smile—"but what does it matter at this late date?"

"The only thing that matters is that I just don't think she's gotten over you."

"You think she's been carrying a torch for me all these years!" Taylor's laugh was one of genuine amusement. "Ridiculous."

"Has she ever had a serious boy friend—since you've known her, I mean?"

"Who knows?"

"Has she ever had anything good to say about any of the women you've taken out?"

"No." Taylor thought a moment. "But in some ways she's like an older sister to me. I don't think it necessarily means she's been jealous of the others. Perhaps she's right—that none of the women I've dated have been right for me." He stood up, crossed over to where Leah sat and smoothed her hair back from her face. "Until I met you, that is." He kissed her on the forehead. "Are we through talking now?"

"Mm-hm."

"Good. Because I have to get some sleep. In three and a half hours, I'm due at a board meeting that might go on all afternoon. Look." He nodded toward the window at the pinkish glow beyond the still-shining lights. "The sun is rising over the city."

"Well—unless you need me at the board meeting," she said with a smile, "I just may sleep the morning away. I don't believe I've ever done that before."

"You probably haven't." He straightened up and started toward his room. "I'm sure it will be good for you."

Leah realized that she was almost too tired to lift her body from where she sat in order to go to her room. The thought ran through her mind that though it had been wonderful and memorable, one such night would be enough to last her a long time. At last, she rose and made her way to her room, a trifle unsteadily. Standing at the foot of the bed, she pulled the straps of the blue dress off her shoulders and let it slide with a silky rustle to the floor. She peeled off her stockings and allowed them, along with the lacy wisps of her underwear, to fall on top of the dress. She stood there a moment, looking downward. *That dress will be ruined,* she thought sleepily, but she had only enough energy to crawl into bed, finding the sheets cool and soft against her skin.

Leah dreamed that she was lying on a sloping beach, at right angles to its length, her feet pointing down toward the sea. At the top of the beach was a room—large, bright, and austere—and in her dream it seemed to be the most beautiful room in the world. She tilted her head back, but she could barely see it, and she stretched her arms over her head, knowing she wanted to be in that room. But the ocean waves were lapping at her ankles; then the water crept higher up her body, and she felt the insistent tug of the tide. She resisted; she was afraid of it, but the sea was warm and sensual, and somehow she wanted to be pulled out to sea, too. And though Taylor was not present in her dream, she knew he had something to do with the sea and that—

There were bells. Or a series of bells ringing sharply. Her eyelids fluttered as she awakened and found that the telephone, which she had placed on the bedside table, was ringing. It must have been ringing for a long time.

She fumbled for the receiver. "Hello," she said sleepily.

She was annoyed when no answering voice came from the other end of the line, only a sharp click, and the connection was broken.

"How rude can people be!" she muttered softly. But she sat up, glad to be awake. She saw that the sun was high in the sky.

Knowing that Taylor was, no doubt, still at his board meeting, she decided not to get dressed right away. She had been smart enough to know that lounging about the suite half dressed would have been an unfair temptation to him. But now that he was not present, she felt like slipping into her robe and slippers and lounging comfortably with the paper for a while. Perhaps she would have room service send up some breakfast.

Or would it be lunch?

Lazily, she picked up the phone and ordered a fruit salad, some rolls and some coffee. She almost laughed as she hung up. She felt like an actress, badly miscast. The part of the city socialite who nightclubbed all night, slept till noon, then ate breakfast in her robe in a luxurious hotel just did not suit her. But it was fun for one morning.

She got out of bed, pulled her robe off her hook and wrapped it about her. *Too bad it's not a silk kimono,* she thought, wrinkling her nose at the blue terry cloth. *And these old slippers should be little pink wedgies with marabou on them.*

She spent an hour with the *Times* as she slowly ate her breakfast. She was just rising to go to her room to dress when there came a double rap on the door.

Could Taylor be back so soon? She had been under the impression that the board meeting would last all day. And here she was, still in her robe!

She had her hand on the doorknob before it dawned on her: why was he knocking when he had a key?

She put her mouth close to the door. "Who is it?" she called tentatively.

"It's Polly Rutherford!"

"Oh!" Leah clutched at her robe in confusion. "If you wouldn't mind waiting a minute—let me throw something on. I'll be right back!"

Cursing softly, she ran to her room, threw off her robe and hastily pulled on her jeans and a sweatshirt. Then, barefoot, she raced back to the door and opened it with shaking hands.

"I'm sorry. Please come in. You see, I was out late last night . . ." Leah let her words trail off. What could she possibly hope to gain by trying to explain herself to Polly? She had a sudden sickening feeling when she thought of the mysterious phone call of an hour before. Polly had wanted to make sure she was really there before she came over. She wondered what it was she wanted to say to her.

"It's quite all right, Leah." Polly was so carefully groomed and made up that she was formidable. The contrast between her appearance and Leah's was almost laughable. Leah was certain that if it were Polly who was staying in the suite, *she* would have a silk kimono to wear! "I had a feeling I'd find you here."

Leah gave a small shrug. There was nothing, absolutely nothing, she could say that would make things look better to Polly. She could almost feel the intensity of Polly's disapproval. Yet, strangely enough, she could see that Polly was trying to smile and be pleasant to her.

"Do you mind if I sit down?"

"Oh, please." Leah gestured toward the sofa.

Polly seated herself on the sofa, and Leah took one of the opposite chairs.

"I just had to talk to you, dear," began Polly.

"Is it about my paintings?" asked Leah nervously.

"I'm afraid not." Polly gave a sad smile. "I do have an appointment with George Mayer tomorrow afternoon—and of course we'll hope for the best. But there's something of even greater importance that I feel I must discuss with you."

"What is it?" Leah was mystified.

Polly leaned forward, a sad little smile on her face, as if she wanted to confide something to Leah— something that would be for Leah's own good.

"How well do you know Taylor Cambridge?" asked Polly gently.

"I haven't known him long," said Leah, "as you probably know. Why do you ask?"

"I'm worried about you, dear."

Leah let no expression cross her face at this astounding remark. "Whatever for?" she asked.

"I myself know Taylor quite well," Polly said, sighing, "as *you* probably know. I hate to see him take advantage of anyone, but especially of a girl as . . . *young* . . . as yourself."

Leah resisted the urge to laugh. She wondered what Polly would think if she knew of all the times Taylor could have taken advantage of her and didn't. "I assure you, Miss Rutherford, there's—"

"Polly."

"Polly, there's nothing to be concerned about."

Polly shook her head. "You probably feel that way because you don't know what I know about Taylor. He's had a parade of young girls with him in this very suite. Unfortunately, you're just one more in a long line of—"

Leah jumped to her feet. "That's none of your affair!" she snapped, her face white with anger. "If that's what you came to tell me, then you might as well leave right now."

"Leah, I'm only trying to help," said Polly in soothing tones. "I know what I'm talking about. I doubt that he's told you that he once had an affair with *me*—and I still regret the day I became involved with him. He never really cared about me."

"He must have been very young!" protested Leah. "People can change—he seems like a caring person. I *know* he's extremely fond of you."

"And is that what *you* want?" Polly's eyes narrowed. "It's not an easy thing to resist falling for Taylor Cambridge. And then, after he's gotten what he wanted, he wants to be your *pal*."

Leah was stricken. She could not ignore the fact that what Polly was saying made a certain amount of sense. It was exactly what she had thought of Taylor when she had first met him.

She sat down slowly. "And do *you* still love him?" she asked compassionately. She suddenly felt a bond with Polly that had not been there before.

"Oh, no." Polly gave a scornful chuckle. "I know him too well for that. I just don't want to see you hurt." She got to her feet. "I have no advice to give you. I just thought a small warning might help you. No, don't get up. I'll see myself out."

Alone in the suite once again, Leah stretched out on the sofa and let her thoughts come as they pleased. She didn't know why Polly's visit had been such a blow to her. What Polly had told her only confirmed what she herself had suspected. Men like Taylor didn't change. It should not be so surprising that he was able to fool her with his controlled passion, his generous concern for her. That was why he was so successful with women. He knew exactly what to do, exactly what to say. He had tried his usual direct approach with Leah, and when she didn't fall for it, he had been forced to resort to subtler and more gallant tactics. She was desperately grateful that she had not yielded to him.

He had said that Polly had been the one to take advantage of him. How could he expect her to believe that? Even as an eighteen-year-old, he must have towered over Polly and outweighed her by sixty pounds at least. And even then he would have been dangerously attractive.

When he walked through the door into the suite later that afternoon, Leah was filled with a confusing mixture of emotions. She had been prepared to hate the sight of him. But he strode in with a glad hello that made her heart miss a beat. His smile seemed utterly and charmingly without guile. Looking healthy and exuberant, he carried his large muscular frame with a light step and seemed happy and at ease. He set his briefcase on the floor near the door, strode over to where Leah stood and planted a kiss on her mouth.

"What a day!" he began. Then Leah saw a look of concern creep into his eyes. He must have felt her stiffness when he kissed her. "Is something wrong?" he asked anxiously.

"No," she said at once. She turned and sat down tensely on the sitting room sofa. She thought quickly. She couldn't possibly tell Taylor about Polly's visit that afternoon. But she had to think of something to explain her uneasy manner—preferably something that was true.

"It's my work," she finally said. Taylor stood in front of her, looking down at her as she spoke. "I feel I have to get back to it. It's been a long time since I've gone this long without doing anything. I suppose what happened with Jacques Léon also has something to do with it. It's like falling off a horse; I feel that I have to get back on right away to prove that I'm not afraid."

Taylor sat beside her and put his arm across her shoulders. How comforting, how good, it felt. "I hate to see you go," he said. "Have you ever thought about painting the city?"

Leah's glance flicked up to meet his eyes. "You mean stay here and work?" She sounded dubious.

"Why not? You and I need to make some kind of decision soon, don't you think? I mean about us."

"Oh, I don't know." She looked away.

"I'm going to be very busy the next few weeks. But it would be nice to have you waiting for me at the end of the day."

Leah smiled briefly. "I'm afraid it would take more than that to keep me happy."

Taylor looked stung. "What do you think I'm

saying?" he demanded. "That I would expect you to knit all day till I came home? I expect you would have a busy life to lead, too. For that matter, I'd be just as happy to wait for you if you were working later than I was. There's nothing I'd like more than to sit on a chair outside your studio door, waiting for you to put the final touch of paint on your masterpiece."

Leah laughed a little at the image. It sounded almost too good to be true. And perhaps that was the heart of the matter. It probably *was* too good to be true. She noticed that he had not made any concrete proposal to her. And she knew that she would not accept it if he did—because of what Polly had told her and also because of her career.

It was just too bad that she was in love with him.

She turned to him and rested her forehead on his shoulder, as if she could draw comfort from the very one who was causing her so much inner turbulence. She wanted to tell him how much he meant to her, how important he was to her. She didn't speak, because the fact remained that her career came first. Of course, Taylor was doing everything he could to advance her career. But she was still afraid. Afraid that with his propensity for taking charge, he might turn her in directions in which she didn't want to go.

She couldn't thrust aside her suspicion that when all was said and done, she was just not that important to him. Perhaps she intrigued him at the moment because she had not been an easy conquest.

How confusing it all was.

"I'd better call the airlines," she said softly. "I'd like to leave tomorrow morning if there's a flight."

"I'll drive you to the airport first thing in the morning, and then my pilot will take you down. No arguments, now." She looked up at him and saw that he was smiling, but the smile didn't crinkle his eyes as much as usual. She reached for his face with her hand and trailed her finger tips along his lean jaw. He sat motionless.

"Well!" he said abruptly, standing up and clapping his hands together once. "I probably should call my pilot now to let him know the plan." He went to the phone, picked up the receiver and began to press the buttons. He paused before he had finished and looked over at Leah from beneath his dark brows. "Say—you wouldn't consider marriage, would you?" he asked.

Leah gave a wry smile. "You give the sorriest proposals of marriage that I've ever heard!" she said, and she hoped she sounded light and teasing. "But even if I thought you meant that, I would have to say no. There's too much uncertainty in my future. And while I'm very grateful to you for trying to help my career—"

"Let's not mention that in the same breath as marriage!" he said sharply, hanging up the phone. "You make it sound as if I offered my help as a kind of bribe."

"I don't really think that." *At least not as a bribe for marriage,* she said to herself. "I just think we ought to take more time. I've been so restless lately, not having done any painting for almost a week. I just have to get back to my work; it will help me think." *Or not to think,* she added silently.

"All right." Taylor shrugged. That shrug said much to Leah. It indicated to her just how unimportant the subject was to him.

He turned back to the phone and called his pilot.

They dined in the hotel dining room that evening.

"Our last meal," quipped Taylor, but it did not seem funny.

They ordered stuffed mushrooms, Caesar salad and

veal. After their wine glasses were filled, Taylor said he would like to propose a special toast.

"Concerning your stay in New York," he said grandly, raising his glass. He looked at her intently. "To your beauty," he said, "and my self-control."

Leah tried to laugh, but she knew this last dinner with Taylor could not be as lighthearted as he seemed to wish. She wondered if they would ever dine together again, if this was truly their last meal together. Certainly she would see him again if their business relationship continued. How difficult that would be for her!

After dinner, they wandered over to the hotel lounge, which had a small dance floor. Leah discovered that Taylor was a superb dancer, allowing her to move gracefully about the floor, held lightly in his arms. The scattered spotlights cast countless shadows on the walls of the small room, and the music was dreamy and subdued. Leah ached with the poignancy of this special time.

"We'd probably do well to turn in early tonight," Taylor said at last in her ear. "We'll be getting up early tomorrow."

Leah nodded, and they took the elevator up to their floor.

Taylor seemed restless when they got inside the room, and he walked about with his hands in his pockets. "I wish you wouldn't go," he said.

Suddenly, Leah was tired of the charade she was playing out. She didn't know if she could really trust Taylor, but she had certainly not tried her best to open up any kind of honest communication between them about what was troubling her.

"Why do you wish that?" she asked from where she sat.

Taylor stopped pacing and regarded her with a

puzzled expression. "I enjoy being with you," he said simply.

"But is that all?" Leah persisted. "Is that the only reason?"

"What are you getting at?" Taylor moved slowly to the chair beside her and seated himself on it.

"It's just that the things you say to me can mean so many different things," Leah said.

Taylor waited expectantly.

"Your admiration for the way I look, your enjoyment of my company, your generosity in helping me, your halfhearted proposals of marriage—"

He looked surprised, but he didn't interrupt.

"—I just wonder how I should interpret all these things. I know there have been many other women in your life. From what I've seen and heard, sometimes I think you're the original playboy . . ."

"Is it your pride, then? Is that what bothers you?"

"No, it's more than that," she answered, turning her face away so he would not see the mist in her eyes.

Taylor bowed his head as if deep in thought. Then he took Leah's chin in his hand and forced her to look at him. "Can you honestly say," he began slowly, "that you know me now and you're still convinced I'm as shallow a person as that? If I felt it would make any sense for me to apologize to you for my past, I would. But can you understand that even that past helps make the impact you've had on me absolutely stunning. What I was . . . makes what you're helping me become . . . even more of a tribute to you. My feeling for you is more now than that first strong attraction I felt."

"Is that true?" She still could not be sure. "I'm still confused."

"I understand," said Taylor, and he pulled her toward him and pressed her against his chest. "Don't worry. I love you, Leah."

His words hung in the air as Leah's heart missed a beat.

"You do?" Her voice was a whisper.

"Yes, I do. I love you from your wonderful mind to your beautiful body, all the way down to your artistic soul. I'd be very happy if you loved me back, but I don't expect it."

Leah pulled back to search his face. It was true; he didn't seem to be demanding anything of her.

A deep, perfect joy welled up within her. So he loved her. And she loved him. That should make everything so simple. But it wasn't simple. She could not make her declaration of love to him just yet. There were too many things she had to think through.

She had no idea of the picture she presented as she gazed at him: her cheeks were flushed with pink, her rosy lips were slightly parted, and her eyes were tender and shining. Taylor leaned forward and kissed her passionately on the mouth.

When the kiss was over, he looked at her quizzically. "I'd like some kind of reaction to what I just told you," he said huskily.

"What you said . . . makes me happy," she faltered.

"But how do *you* feel?"

"I don't know."

"Oh, come now. Either you love me or you don't love me!"

"No, Taylor." Leah shook her head. "It's not that simple. You'll have to give me some time to think about it."

"I can wait. As long as I know I have a chance." His tone changed. "Are you still going back to Vero?"

"Oh, yes." She reached up to caress his face.

"When will I see you again?"

Leah withdrew her hand and sighed. "I don't know," she murmured.

Taylor held her quietly in his arms for a long time.

Chapter Nine

The pilot of Taylor's plane helped Leah out of the craft and offered to drive her to the Ocean Inn. He dropped her off in the parking lot; she insisted that she could carry her light suitcase up to her room herself.

When she opened the door to her room, she was touched by an empty feeling. Most of her completed paintings had been removed, to be offered up, she knew, to the cold scrutiny of some distant gallery owners.

There was nothing to be done but to create more.

She combed her hair out, looking thoughtfully in the mirror as she did so. She wasn't in the mood to take up her paintbrush immediately, so she decided to go over to the gallery. If Rhoda wasn't there, she would call her later. She went out to her car. When she turned the key in the ignition, the engine grated alarmingly, but it finally caught, and Leah eased the car out of the parking lot.

When she entered the low boxlike building that was the gallery, Leah saw that the show was in the process of being dismantled. Some of the rooms were completely empty. Others contained people who were taking down paintings and packing them up for removal. Leah went to the room where her paintings had been displayed and found that the walls were bare.

She turned to leave the room and ran into Rhoda Hughes in the hall.

"Leah, you're back!"

"Hello, Rhoda!" She fell into step beside Rhoda, who was headed toward one of the back rooms. "Rhoda, did someone buy my other painting?"

"Yes." Rhoda's eyes twinkled. "I did."

"Oh, dear. I hope you didn't feel you had—"

"Nonsense, Leah! I *love* that painting of yours! My husband and I are thrilled to have it hanging on our wall."

"Well, I'm rather thrilled myself," said Leah, "that you liked it so much."

"We promise we'll give it a good home." She eyed Leah. "How was the trip to New York?"

"Well . . . are you free to talk about it over lunch?"

Before Rhoda could answer, a lady came up behind her and grabbed her arm. "Hurry, Rhoda," she said. "The van is leaving now. We need your help."

"Oh, I must run," said Rhoda. "Leah, I won't be able to make it for lunch, but I have a much better idea. Please join us for dinner tonight. My daughter is in town, and I'd love for the two of you to meet. She's going to be married! And I want you to meet my husband, of course, and to see your painting in its new home."

"That sounds wonderful!" said Leah, her acceptance heartfelt. She was relieved to have plans for the evening. She had felt edgy all morning and knew she wouldn't be as content as she usually was if she had to spend the evening alone.

"Please come at seven," said Rhoda. She quickly wrote her address on a piece of paper, handed it to Leah, then dashed off with her friends.

There was no further reason to stay at the gallery, so Leah drove back to the hotel. She went up to her room and started to change into her bathing suit, but stopped when she caught a glimpse of her body in the mirror. She looked at its pale bisque color with distaste. Suddenly, the light tan she had acquired a week before did not please her. She decided to be a little more earnest about getting a tan, as most Florida visitors were. She was struck with the desire for a new bathing suit—a bikini, to be exact, which would allow the largest amount of skin to be exposed to the sun.

She put her jeans and shirt back on and went down the stairs, across the parking lot and out to the street. The sun was almost blinding, and the temperature was close to ninety, but Leah enjoyed the baking heat. She crossed the street to look in the windows of the small touristy shops that lined the street opposite the Ocean Inn. She picked one that had bright casual wear prominently displayed and entered its air-conditioned interior.

"May I help you, dear?" A small gray-haired lady trotted forth.

"I'd like to try on swim suits."

The saleslady gestured toward the racks of brilliantly colored swim wear. "Please help yourself. The dressing room is right over there."

Leah examined the rows of swim wear. Her hand strayed toward a black bikini, but then she remembered that Taylor liked her in bright colors. She pulled out several suits, a turquoise one, a bright red, a hot pink and several multicolored ones. She took the handful of tiny knit garments to the dressing room and closed the curtain.

She almost laughed out loud when she tried on the first one. Made of a thin clingy material, it was so brief that the top barely contained her. The bottom half was a pair of ridiculously small triangles tied together at the sides with strings.

"Is everything going all right?" The saleslady's voice floated in from outside the dressing room.

"Just fine," sang out Leah as she shimmied out of the first bikini and reached for another one.

She tried on several more that did not satisfy her, but when she had the pink one on, she paused a little longer in front of the mirror. It was as brief as some of the others, but she knew immediately that it was extremely becoming. The top was plain and had two thin straps that tied at the neck; it was cut low so that her breasts swelled gently above the fabric. The bottom half was cut very high in front, in the new fashion, so that her long legs appeared to be even longer. She turned about, undecided.

"Do you need some help, dear?"

Leah opened the curtain, feeling she needed a second opinion.

"You look terrific!" exclaimed the woman with sincere admiration.

"Do you think it's too daring?" asked Leah.

"It is daring—but perfect. Most people couldn't wear something like that." She turned to a rack behind her and pulled out a ruffled white cotton cover-up with floral splashes of the same hot pink as the suit. "This was made to go with it."

Leah fell in love with the feminine look of the cover-up. "I'll take it all," she said quickly before she could have second thoughts.

She walked back to her room with her shopping bag of purchases. She snacked on a single orange that was still in her room from before she left for New York. She smoothed some protective sun-tan lotion over her fair skin and put on her new bikini and cover-up. Then she picked up her hat, sketch pad and charcoal and headed down the stairs and to the beach.

She sketched for less than an hour before she set her sketch pad aside. She spread out her beach towel, removed her hat and cover-up and lay back on the towel, face turned to the sun. The sounds of children playing in the surf seemed to recede slightly, and she felt drowsiness creep up on her.

She wasn't sure how long she had lain there before a sudden diminishing of the light that penetrated her eyelids made her aware that someone was blocking the sun. Her eyes flew open to see a tanned masculine form standing over her, his feet just inches from her shoulder.

She sat up hastily and squinted upward.

"Hi there," he said, with a greeting that was obviously intended to be smooth and offhand. He was a young man, probably about twenty, blond. "I'm Eric. What's your name?" As he spoke, he squatted down beside her till his eyes were looking directly into hers.

"Leah," she replied noncommittally and waited to see if he had a legitimate reason for disturbing her sun bath.

He shifted his position till he was sitting Indian

style, his back rounded, his face held a little too close
to hers, she thought. "I saw you lying here all by
yourself, and I thought I'd introduce myself," he said
ingenuously. "Like to go out?"

Out of the corner of her eye, Leah noticed two
other tanned, tow-headed young men standing some
distance off. They were watching her encounter with
Eric, who was obviously a friend of theirs. "No, thank
you," she said. She made a move to lie back on the
towel, certain that the youthful Eric would be easily
scared away.

But he persisted. "There's a party tonight and—"

"No, thank you. I don't date."

He looked at her with astonishment. "You're kid-
ding!" She saw that he was having trouble keeping his
eyes on her face, that they kept dropping to her bikini
top. She considered reaching for her cover-up and
putting it on, but she really wished he would just go
away and leave her alone. He seemed to have no
intention of leaving. "What do you do for fun?" he
asked.

She gave him a sour look.

"I thought we could spend some time together," he
went on. "You're a good-looking lady—"

Leah had the impression that he was being silently
egged on by his friends, and she was growing tired
of the game. She draped her cover-up over her
shoulders, gathered up the rest of her things and
stood.

"I really have to go now," she said. "I have a lot to
do." She turned to walk the short distance to the
hotel.

Eric was but a breath behind her. "Did you come
down with some friends?" he asked. "My friends and
I plan to spend a lot of time on this beach—we could
be here when you come back."

Leah shook her head.

"Well, if it's just you, then," he went on, "my friends could find some other girls. I could wait here for you if you'll be back soon."

Leah turned to face the young man, realizing that the usual off-putting tactics would not work with him. She didn't wish to be unkind, so she said the only thing that she thought he would understand. "I'm in love with someone," she said. "I'm engaged. So you see, I can't go out with you." Her voice caught in her throat when she realized that at least part of what she said was true. It was the first time she had put her feelings into words—Eric, the young beachcomber, was the first to know that she was in love.

"Oh, okay. Sure. No offense," he said.

"None taken." She watched him turn and rejoin his friends on the beach.

She continued on to her room, feeling relieved and troubled at the same time. She sat down on the edge of the bed and stared at the floor for many long minutes.

"I'm in love with Taylor," she said out loud for a second time, and a warm shiver passed through her body at this admission. "What shall I do?"

Once again, she acknowledged to herself that there was no easy answer. In spite of Taylor's forthright declaration, she still had nagging doubts that he really loved her. And what if he did love her and wanted her to marry him? A part of her wanted that, but another part of her clung to her old belief that marriage would put an end to her painting, that her sacrifice would be too great. She was probably as weak as her sister, she thought with a touch of scorn for them both. Once faced with the heady options of wealth, her devotion to her work might possibly fly right out the window.

No! she told herself, clenching her fists. *I won't let that become a possibility.*

She felt a desperate need to talk to somebody. She thought about calling Rhoda or her mother. She even considered dialing Eve's number in Dallas. But she was afraid she might not have the nerve to bring up the subject that occupied her so fully, and she dreaded the superficial conversation that would result. Instead, she dragged out paints, brushes, and a half-finished canvas and set determinedly to work.

At six o'clock, she started cleaning up and getting dressed, and a few minutes after seven, she was pulling up in front of the white towerlike building that contained Rhoda's condominium. She entered the lobby and went to the wall that contained the rows of mail compartments and name plates. She pressed the button located next to the Hughes name.

"Come right up, Leah." Rhoda's voice crackled over the intercom. "I've unlocked the entrance door; come on up to the second floor."

Leah walked through the large double doors that separated the lobby from the rest of the building and took the elevator to Rhoda's floor. She stepped out into the hall and saw that one of the doors was open. Rhoda was standing in the doorway, and she beckoned to Leah with a gracious gesture.

"Come on in," she said, and Leah followed her inside. "I'll introduce you to your painting first."

They went immediately to the living room, and the first thing Leah noticed was a pair of French doors that opened out onto a balcony that overlooked the sea. The furniture in the room was beautifully traditional, its lines softened by a potted Ficus tree, a large Boston fern and several other leafy plants. Then, on the left, Leah saw the large, smooth wall where her painting was hung. The wall was painted a medium dark shade of brown; against it, the paler beiges of the painting stood out in bold relief, and the pinks and blues in it seemed to spring to life.

"It's perfect!" said Leah spontaneously; then she felt a little abashed at her admiration for her own work in its new setting. But she saw with a glance at her friend that Rhoda was pleased with her reaction. "You didn't have the wall painted that color especially to show off the painting, did you?"

"No, as a matter of fact, I didn't. I've always enjoyed decorating with that color. It shows certain works of art off to perfection."

"It's stunning against the white molding," commented Leah, her eyes traveling about the room. They came to rest on a doorway where two figures, a man and a woman, had suddenly appeared. The young woman was small and attractive, with short auburn hair, and the man, obviously her father, stood beside her with his arm draped protectively over her shoulders.

"Leah, this is my daughter, Debby, and my husband, Jim. And, of course"—she gestured toward Leah—"this is our favorite artist, Leah DuChaine."

"I'm so glad to meet you," said Debby with a sparkling smile. "I've been hinting to mother that your painting would make a perfect wedding gift."

"You'd better forget that idea," said her father good-naturedly. "Your mother loves that painting too much."

Jim Hughes, of solid build and with gray hair, was quite a bit older than Rhoda. He seemed calm and quiet, a good foil for the livelier personalities of his wife and daughter.

"Congratulations on your happy news," said Leah, directing her remark to Rhoda's daughter.

Debby's lips curved into a happy smile. "Thank

you. It is wonderful, isn't it? I think mother and father were beginning to wonder if I would ever get married."

"Oh, yes," said Rhoda in a bantering tone. "Still single at the ripe old age of twenty-three! Your father and I thought we would have you on our hands forever!" She paused a moment to reflect. "Not that we've seen very much of you in the last five years!"

"Mother, getting an education is time consuming!" Debby protested. "The academic work was a breeze, but all those mixers—" She shook her head in mock weariness. "Finding the right man takes a lot of endurance!"

Leah laughed at Debby's candid remark. She found herself liking the younger woman, though she doubted that they had very much in common.

"Why don't we sit in the living room for a while?" suggested Rhoda. "Jim's made his special frozen daiquiris, and the dinner will take care of itself for a while."

Once seated, Debby asked Leah a few polite questions about the life of an artist, but when Leah began to question her about her fiancé, she seemed much more eager to talk—about him and about their wedding plans. She said that her fiancé had wanted to come to Florida with her to meet her parents but that he had just started a new job as an electrical engineer and wouldn't be able to travel down from Philadelphia till sometime later.

"It's a good job," said Debby, apparently quite impressed with her husband-to-be. "It's not easy getting work right out of school. Thank goodness we can go ahead with the wedding as planned. We might have had to delay it if Mark hadn't found work."

Leah wasn't sure why Debby and her fiancé seemed

to be almost children to her. She was not too much older than they, and she certainly didn't consider herself to be very worldly or sophisticated. But Debby's concerns seemed simpler, and her dreams seemed uncomplicated and well within her reach.

They conversed for a while longer, the Hughes family stopping once or twice to admire Leah's painting again, till the soft ping of a bell sounded from the kitchen.

"Oh, that's our dinner!" said Rhoda, starting up. "We must go to the table immediately. I've always wanted to serve a soufflé before it sank," she confided to Leah as she hurried past her into the kitchen.

Rather than going directly to the dining room, Jim, Debby and Leah followed Rhoda into the kitchen to help. There was much laughter as they got in one another's way, tripping over each other in their hurry to get the food on the table.

"I feel as if I've just run a race," breathed Rhoda when they were all seated at last. The meal was composed of roast chicken, a large salad, bread and a magnificent spinach soufflé.

"I haven't seen such a meal since the last time Debby was here to visit," said Jim gruffly.

"Oh, you big tease!" said Rhoda. "You've seen plenty of meals like this!" Then, thoughtfully, she added, "Of course, most of them have been meals we've had in restaurants."

"That's more like it!" said Debby approvingly. "Why should the man retire and take it easy while the woman continues to slave in the kitchen?"

Her father said nothing, but gave her an amused look.

"Leah, you must tell us about your trip to New York," invited Rhoda.

A look at Rhoda's face assured Leah that her friend was not urging her to reveal everything. Leah told them of some of the restaurants and museums she had been to while in the city, and then she explained that she had a friend who was putting forth some effort to get her work represented in a good art gallery.

"How thrilling!" exclaimed Rhoda, clasping her hands together.

"That's wonderful," agreed Debby. "I hope I'll get a chance to see some more of your work someday. Perhaps Mark will take me to New York sometime . . . after we're married . . ."

Leah gave Debby a sympathetic smile. She just hoped that Debby was as much in love with her husband-to-be as she was in love with the idea of marriage. She watched the young woman as the meal progressed. Her face and manner were very youthful, yet she had that supreme self-confidence that sometimes accompanies naïveté. Leah learned that Debby planned to work, probably in retailing, after her marriage, but the job was not important to her in itself. Rather, it seemed to be a way of giving Debby something to do—*until the children come along,* thought Leah, smiling to herself. At once her mind began to wander down another path as she considered Debby's personal relationship with her fiancé. She wondered if this fresh-faced girl felt her pulse quicken when her fiancé entered the room, if she longed for him in the way Leah herself longed for Taylor, if she quivered at his touch—

Leah actually blushed at the turn her thoughts had taken and was relieved to see that nobody seemed to notice. She couldn't help comparing herself with Debby. Their differences were apparent—she wondered what, as women, they had in common.

"When will the wedding be?" asked Leah.

"December twentieth, in Minnesota, where I grew up," said Debby, and she spoke of bridesmaids dressed in cranberry-red velvet and a church festooned with garlands of greenery.

After dessert, coffee and more conversation, Leah rose to take her leave. She thanked Rhoda for the delicious dinner and for allowing her to meet her family. She wished Debby luck and smilingly bid Jim Hughes farewell.

"And Leah," said Rhoda softly as she showed Leah to the door, "Debby's leaving tomorrow morning, so why don't you and I have lunch about twelve? We can talk then."

"Thank you," said Leah gratefully, and she pressed Rhoda's hand.

When Leah got back to her room at the Ocean Inn, she undressed and lay down on the bed to think. She felt disturbed as she thought over the events of the previous few days. Meeting Rhoda's daughter and seeing her excitement over her wedding had affected Leah in a strange way. It had stirred up her thoughts and emotions, had caused her to examine her feelings and ask herself what she truly wanted. She felt another sudden strong urge to call her sister Eve.

She glanced at the clock. Eleven o'clock. That meant it was still only ten o'clock in Dallas and probably a good time to call, because young Andrew would have been bathed and put to bed long before then.

She swung herself out of bed, walked to the phone and dialed Eve's number, not knowing exactly what she wanted to say to her sister.

"Leah!" Eve sounded delighted. A sudden sharp image of her sister appeared in Leah's mind at the sound of Eve's voice, which was so like her own. Eve, though blonde like Leah, had hair the color of honey rather than pale silver; her complexion was dark, and her beautiful eyes were almond shaped and brown. Both sisters were beautiful, but in very different ways. "I can't believe it's really you!"

"I'm calling from Florida," said Leah. "I've been on a kind of working vacation. How's Jerry? And Andy?"

The sisters chatted and discussed Eve's family for a while. Then, hesitantly, Leah turned to the subject that was on her mind. "I need some advice, Eve. I find myself in a . . . situation . . . similar to the one you found yourself in five years ago."

"Oh?" Eve's tone was suddenly guarded.

"I'm in love," said Leah carefully. "And I would like to ask you something. Are you alone?"

"Yes."

"Eve"—she plunged right in—"do you regret marrying and having a child rather than pursuing your career in art?" As soon as she spoke the words, she wished she could call them back. "I'm sorry. That was insensitive. You don't have to—"

"Oh, no, that's quite all right." Eve laughed softly. "It sounds as if you have a very good reason for wanting to know." She took a breath. "Leah, I would not be truthful if I told you that I never have any regrets. But Jerry loves me, and I love him. And we love our child; oh, you won't know how much till you have one of your own. I don't think that any amount of satisfaction in a career can take the place of that. I have a good life, Leah, a very good life."

"I'm happy for you, Eve," said Leah simply. But she had really wanted to know more than that. She wanted to know why Eve had lost her drive to develop her talent after she had married. She wanted to know if Eve thought it was impossible to be a wife and mother *and* an artist. But she sensed that she couldn't ask her these questions; she was afraid it might sound as if she were criticizing her sister.

"Do you really love this man?" Eve asked.

"Yes," said Leah, very aware of the confidence in her voice.

"My advice would be: Don't let him get away. But of course the decision is yours."

"Thanks, Eve," said Leah warmly. "You've really helped." She wanted her sister to think that she really had helped.

"Oh—I always advise going for the happy-ever-after ending," Eve joked. Then she said in a confidential tone, "Leah, I have done a little painting lately. A few water-colors, some things for Andy's room. It was fun."

"That's great," said Leah approvingly. "I love you, Eve."

"I love you, too."

Leah felt a trace of sadness after she hung up the phone. She was honestly glad that Eve had so much happiness in her life, but she couldn't shake her conviction that Eve herself felt that she was missing something, something important.

But Leah's thoughts turned back quickly to her own problems. Nothing that had happened during the day had made things any clearer to her; nothing had helped her decide what she must do.

I need to talk to Rhoda, she decided, and she wanted to call her immediately. But of course it was much too late; the next day would have to do.

She threw herself on the bed again, trying to force herself to concentrate. She wondered who could help her. The frightening thought occurred to her that perhaps no one could help her. For a few minutes, she allowed herself to get used to the thought, and then she began to wonder if it was so frightening, after all. Even Eve had said it: No one could make her decisions for her. Only she herself could do that.

She tried to make her decision simple. She badly wanted two things that seemed to be mutually exclusive. She had always wanted to be an artist and had set about working for that goal with a rare determination. But now there was a love that she wanted just as badly—

Just as badly? With sudden insight, she realized that her career ambition had grown somewhat paler when she compared it with her love for Taylor. Wonder of wonders, she wanted Taylor even more than she wanted her career. How foolish it would be to toss aside a new-found love because of vague fears—fears that she *might* lose interest in her career, that she *might* find a life with Taylor too distracting. If her love wasn't worth taking risks for, then it really wasn't much of a love at all.

"I want him more than anything," she said aloud with quiet exultation. At this moment of understanding, she thought her heart would burst.

The thought occurred to her that even aside from the tangible help he seemed bent on giving her, a life with Taylor might be a boon for her career. Perhaps his belief in her, his very confidence in her, would make all the difference.

She looked at the clock again. It was a few minutes after midnight. It would be the same time in New York. Should she wait till morning to call him?

The answer, of course, was no, she should not wait. If Taylor's feelings for her were genuine—a stab of fear raced through her, but she forced herself to continue her thought—then he would want her to call him no matter what the hour.

But first she called the airport and talked for several minutes to the ticket agent.

Afterward, she dialed the number Taylor had given her, holding her breath.

"Hello." His voice was not fogged with sleep as she had expected.

"Taylor—I hope I didn't wake you."

"No, Leah, I was awake," he said quickly. She tried to listen for a recognizable emotion in his voice but heard none.

"Has anything interesting happened since I left?" She knew she was just stalling for time.

"No," he said briefly. Then his tone grew intense. "Leah, do you have something to tell me?"

Leah found herself clutching the receiver tightly, as if she held on for dear life. "Yes," she whispered. She tried out several phrases in her mind that would express what she wanted to say and then decided on the simple truth. "I love you."

Time stood still. Taylor said nothing, but sighed heavily as Leah's heart plummeted.

"Taylor. Was that a glad sound or—or not?"

"Oh, Leah—I've dreamed of this. I thought you had some feeling for me, but I knew I was competing with something else in your life. And for the last couple of days I thought I had lost." His voice was warm and deep. "I love you, Leah."

At once, Leah was exhilarated again. Her words came out in a rush. "I'm willing to make sacrifices that I wouldn't have considered before," she said. "My priorities are different now—"

"Leah, don't you understand?" Taylor broke in. "I don't want you to give up a thing! All I want is for you to be mine and love me. I'll fight as hard as I expect you will for the time you can devote to your painting. And Leah"—something boyish crept into his tone—"now we can get married!"

Leah's reply was a dissatisfied groan.

"What's the matter?" demanded Taylor anxiously.

"This is the third time now," Leah scolded.

"Oh, I see what you mean. My marriage proposals do leave a little something to be desired, don't they? I'm sorry, honey. I promise you, when you get here, I'll give you the finest marriage proposal I can think of . . ." His words trailed off into silence. "But Leah—"

"Yes?"

"What do you think your answer will be?"

"I think you know already."

"Then I won't be disappointed?"

"No, you won't," she said softly.

"When are you coming to New York?" he asked.

"I'd like to come day after tomorrow." Her voice grew uncertain. "Is that all right?"

"I was going to ask you to come tomorrow!"

"I would, but—I have a few loose ends to tie up around here."

"I'll have my plane sent—"

"There's no need," she informed him. "I already have a reservation on a commercial flight. It gets into LaGuardia at eleven-fifty."

He whistled with admiration. "And have you made plans for your car?"

"I was wondering—could I leave it at your beach house for now?"

"Great idea. I'll phone Nelson tomorrow. And he can drive you to the airport."

"I'll be leaving very early—before six."

"I don't believe Nelson will mind."

"Taylor—there's one more thing. Did Polly show the paintings to George Mayer yet?"

"Yes."

From the silence that followed, Leah knew that the news was not good. But she was too happy to care.

"That's all right," she said. "Good-by, my love."

"Good-by, love."

Chapter Ten

The next day, Leah had a relaxed and cheerful lunch with Rhoda on the patio of the hotel. Rhoda was filled with questions, but she laughed when she realized that Leah's state of mind was happy and peaceful.

"It appears to me that something's happened to you!" she observed. "You're different than you were at our house last night."

"Could you tell something was wrong?" asked Leah.

Rhoda snorted. "I could see that under your usual calm exterior there was turmoil. You wanted to talk to me alone, didn't you—and yet you seemed fascinated with what my daughter had to say about her upcoming marriage."

"I did?" Leah looked sheepish.

"Yes, and I knew it wasn't the usual polite interest in the event," she said wisely. "Now tell me. What did you do after you got home last night?"

"I made a few phone calls," said Leah in an offhand manner.

Rhoda waited expectantly.

"I called my sister in Dallas," Leah went on. "We had a nice chat."

Rhoda nodded.

"Then I called the airport."

"Mm-hm."

"Then—I called Taylor in New York. I told him that I love him, he said he loves me, and I told him I'd be up to see him in two days." Leah sat back triumphantly, her blue eyes sparkling.

Rhoda rested her chin on her fist and looked at her young friend with a serene smile. "That doesn't sound too complicated."

Leah rolled her eyes. "Oh, if you only knew—"

"I think I do understand, Leah. It can't have been as easy as it sounds. Well, let me be the first to congratulate you."

"Thank you. I'll let you know when the wedding will be."

"Oh, so he has proposed!"

"Yes . . . in a manner of speaking. Although I haven't actually accepted . . . at least not in so many words."

Rhoda laughed. "I'm not worried about you," she said. "Now, how about some of this wonderful crab salad?"

That afternoon, Leah found Joyce at the reception desk and thanked her for her wonderful stay, promising to return. She decided to check out, explaining that she would be leaving very early the next morning.

She felt a little wistful as she sat alone in one of the deck rocking chairs that evening, enjoying the ocean view. Already she knew that the little town of Vero Beach would always be a magic place to her: *This is where Taylor and I met.* She laughed quietly, remembering that first meeting. Things had certainly changed since then. She hoped they would return often to Vero Beach.

The next morning, Leah woke before dawn and put on her old blue-gray linen dress and sandals. She quickly packed the rest of her clothes in her suitcase. She decided to carry her art supplies in their burlap bag on the plane, except for the remaining canvases, which she would lock in the trunk of her car till she and Taylor returned.

She carried everything down to her car, then went back to her room to lock it for the last time. She smiled secretly as she turned the key in the lock. She believed she was the only one awake in the inn. She alone could hear the whispering of the sea, could feel the breezes stir her hair. And within was the even more delightful stirring of anticipation.

It was a short drive to Taylor's beach house. Leah grew a little nervous when she turned into the driveway, as no lights were visible in the house. She realized that she probably should have made contact with the Nelsons the day before just to make sure that they understood her plans. She hoped that Taylor had been able to reach them.

She started up the walk. As she approached the front door, she was relieved to see a faint glow through the curtained window, which meant that a light was on in the hall. The door opened before she even had a chance to knock. There stood Nelson, professional as always, ready to go.

The sun rose during the trip to the airport. Leah watched it through the window of the car, feeling her heart rise along with it. She was grateful for Nelson's silence, which allowed her to be alone with her thoughts. She tried to impress every detail of the Floridian landscape on her mind. She knew that the pale colors and the vegetation in mellow shades of green would forever be associated with pleasurable excitement. At times, for a second or two, she would force herself to think about something besides Taylor, though she was still aware of the strong undercurrent of happiness within her. Then thoughts of him would flash into her consciousness again, and she would try to hide her smiles so that Nelson would not think he was chauffeuring a grinning idiot.

Nelson carried Leah's suitcase to the ticket counter. He waited while she purchased her ticket, wished her luck with a wooden expression that almost made her laugh, then left to return home. Leah wondered when she would get to meet the mysterious Mrs. Nelson and wondered if she were more talkative than her husband.

The plane made a short stop in Orlando. It was a little before noon when it finally touched down at LaGuardia Airport.

Leah's fantasies of throwing herself into Taylor's arms the moment she stepped off the plane were dashed when she strolled out of the passageway leading from the plane to the airport. She had forgotten that for security reasons friends and relatives awaiting disembarking passengers were no longer permitted to wait at the gates. She set off down the seemingly endless hall with the other passengers, who were determinedly marching toward the baggage-claim area.

She spied the security station and, just beyond, a group of officials who manned the low gates that held back the waiting crowd. She saw Taylor immediately, his height making him easy to spot in the crowd. Her heart turned over at the sight of him.

He seemed a trifle irritated as she approached him. "They wouldn't let me through to meet you," he groused. "They told me I would have to apply for a special pass. I told them you were a very small girl and would have a huge bag of heavy supplies that you would need help with, but it didn't seem to make any difference to them."

Leah smiled at his concern and allowed her moderately heavy bag to slide to the floor with a thump as Taylor enfolded her in his arms. He pulled her against him violently, then held her as if completely unaware of the press of people around them. For a long moment, they stood that way, Taylor holding the lean length of his body against hers as if he meant to leave his imprint on her, to mark her as his own. She clung to him, reveling in his warmth and clean scent, in the feel of his hard muscles, in the knowledge that she felt happy and excited and unafraid in his arms. Only after the embrace did he bend to touch her lips with his own. When at last they broke apart, Leah looked up at him with a breathless smile.

"So I'm a very small girl, am I?"

Taylor shook his head. "My mistake, madam." He grabbed her hand possessively. "Let's get your bag and find the limo."

As they started off, Leah noticed that a few grins and winks were thrown their way.

They were in for a tedious wait at the baggage-claim area, but nothing could be so frustrating that it could keep them from exchanging smiles.

After they picked up Leah's suitcase, they went to find the waiting black limousine with its patient driver. They sat close together in the spacious interior, Taylor with his arm around Leah's waist.

They made small talk for a few minutes. Leah told

Taylor of Rhoda's purchase of her painting and how she had been to her house and had seen it hanging on the wall. She asked him about his work. She didn't bring up the subject of Polly and the art dealers, wanting him to make first mention of that. But then she realized that Taylor was not giving his full attention to her.

"I'm sorry to be rattling on so," she said with a little laugh. "You look as if there's something on your mind. Is everything all right?"

"Yes, of course."

But he said nothing more. Finally, she asked him teasingly, "Aren't you impressed with how I've managed to avoid the subject that I'm dying to discuss?"

She could not fathom the look that came into Taylor's eyes. He said carefully, "We've had no response from George Mayer as yet. I wouldn't give up hope, though. These things take time."

"I suppose so," she said. "I was surprised when Jacques Léon responded so promptly." She thought Taylor looked a little concerned. "Please don't worry about me. I'm very good at waiting. You just watch. You won't believe how cool I can be."

"That's good. Because I'd like you to give your attention to something else right now." He reached into his inside coat pocket and withdrew a flat longish box. Leah eyed it curiously. It didn't seem the proper shape or size to contain an engagement ring.

"It's for you," said Taylor, handing her the box. "A gift."

Leah opened the box and drew in her breath softly at the sight of the beautiful bracelet that sparkled against midnight-blue velvet. Its delicate links were sterling silver, and four large glittering diamonds were spaced along its length.

"It's gorgeous," breathed Leah. "Thank you." She looked up to see Taylor studying her, a curious smile on his lips.

"Very interesting," he remarked.

"What?"

"Your reaction. Do you know I was almost afraid to get it for you?"

"Why?"

"Well, I know how you feel about such things. I've tried buying gifts for you before; don't you remember? And my good intentions came to nothing. I was hoping—"

"Taylor Cambridge, don't be ridiculous! Don't pretend that you don't understand! I *will* give this bracelet right back if you keep this up. You know things have changed."

Taylor smiled into her flashing eyes. "Yes, things *have* changed," he said. "And I've always wanted to buy you diamonds." He lifted the bracelet out of its box and fastened it about Leah's wrist. It fit closely and sparkled as she turned her hand about. "It looks beautiful on you."

"It is beautiful," she agreed, and she kissed him sweetly on the mouth.

He caught her in his arms and looked into her eyes. "I wonder if it's the proper moment," he murmured. "Yes, I believe it is." His eyes were alight with love. "Leah DuChaine," he said in measured tones, "I love you deeply. Nothing would make me happier than if you would consent to be at my side forever. Will you be my wife?"

"Yes," she whispered. Any further words she might have spoken were made unnecessary by the sharing of a long, fervent kiss.

As they pulled apart, Leah saw a hint of mischief in

Taylor's eye. "How was that for a proposal?" he asked.

"Much . . . better," she observed. She glanced out the window and noticed for the first time that they were taking a route not familiar to her. "We're not going to the hotel?"

"No, not this time. I want to show you where I live."

"And am I to meet the houseful of guests, too?" she asked, shrinking a bit.

"No, indeed. Every last one of the guests has departed. And I have invited only one new one, a person I very much want you to meet."

"Who is that?"

Taylor shot her a sideways glance. "My mother."

"I'll be delighted to meet her," she said warmly.

"And when my father gets back from overseas, you can meet him, too. I grew up in the house I'm taking you to. When my parents decided to move into a condominium several years ago, they sold it to me. My mother will probably be there when we arrive. It's really very fortunate that she could come." He looked at her. "She has the engagement ring. You see, it belonged to her grandmother, who had decided that the bride of one of her great-grandsons should wear it someday. My cousins are all much younger than I am, so it was always assumed that my wife would wear it. When my great-grandmother died, my mother kept the ring safe for me. She gave it to me when I was twenty-one." He sighed. "She took it back when I was thirty."

Leah laughed. "So she gave up on you?"

"She certainly did. My three cousins were barely in their teens, but she swore one of them would be married before I was. But I've surprised her. She'll be thrilled to see you wear it, Leah."

"I hope so," she said quietly. "Do you think she'll like me, Taylor?"

"Of course she'll like you. She'll love you! She's an art lover, but she'll feel drawn to you for other reasons, too. Not the least of which is that you make her son happy."

Leah smiled.

"She, too, was a great beauty in her day."

"You're not saying I'm a great beauty, are you!" Leah said with a touch of genuine annoyance.

"Yes, I am," he replied in a tone that brooked no argument. "Even Mother's coloring was similar to yours—very fair. Her hair is white now—but it's a lovely silver white, and I think she's still beautiful." He squeezed Leah's hand. "Really, you have nothing to fear from her. I've told her about you, so she knows you're wonderful."

Leah smiled and shook her head. How could she possibly live up to Taylor's praises of her? "What did you tell her about me?" she asked.

Taylor held her close to him and spoke into her ear. "Oh, I told her a whole list of things. I just wish we were alone right now so I could recite them for you."

"That's not why you want to be alone with me!" Leah said, laughing as she extricated herself from his embrace.

"I suppose we'll have to make some definite plans," said Taylor. He glanced out the window. They were now traveling through the upper East Side, with its fashionable cooperatives and condominiums. They made a turn on to a side street, which was lined with elegant brownstones. He turned back to Leah. "Will your mother insist on a big traditional wedding with all the frills?"

"Of course," Leah said without hesitation.

"And I suppose it must be held in Charlotte."

"Where else?" she asked Leah, her blue eyes wide and innocent. "What other American city has enough beauty and charm to be the proper setting for the perfect wedding?"

Taylor sighed. "I'm really anxious to get this done," he confessed. "I don't suppose a week would give your mother enough time to arrange things?"

"You'll have to give her a month at least."

Taylor sighed again, but there was good-natured resignation in his eyes. Leah knew that he would endure the old-style festivities in her home town with grace and good humor, and she loved him for it.

The limousine slowed, pulled over to one side of the street and came to a stop beside the endless line of cars parked by the curb.

"This is it." Taylor nodded toward his house as the driver retrieved Leah's suitcase from the back, then opened their door. Leah had an impression of some lacy-branched small trees that were scattered in front of a row of attached brownstones that looked as if they dated from the turn of the century. Taylor's house was a magnificent three-story brownstone with leaded windows and a carved-oak front door.

Leah and Taylor took time for one last warm, lingering kiss before they started up the front walk.

Chapter Eleven

Taylor's mother was petite and dressed in powder blue. Taylor had said she was sixty, but her face looked very youthful. A servant was at the door when Taylor and Leah entered the house, but right behind him was Mrs. Cambridge, gracious and smiling. Her silver hair really was beautiful, and she wore it softly curled about her face.

Mrs. Cambridge gave her son a perfunctory kiss on the cheek, then hurried around to Leah, whose hands she took in both of her own. "Leah DuChaine," she said. "You're as pretty as my son said you were." She raised up a little bit on her toes to give Leah a welcoming kiss. "We'll be proud to have you as part of our family."

"Mrs. Cambridge, thank you so much. I'm so happy to be here," said Leah, hoping she wasn't being too effusive.

"She's just charming," the older woman said to her son, as if she were praising Leah's slightly flustered manner. She gave Leah time to freshen herself up after her journey, then led her, along with Taylor, into a large room she called the drawing room.

Unlike Taylor's Florida beach house with its contemporary feel, the room looked as if it contained things that had been in existence for centuries. The furniture was mahogany, dark and lustrous, and the heavy draperies and upholstered pieces were in shades of dusky blue and rose. A collection of elegant crystal decanters containing various cordials rested on a small credenza. Leah's eyes rested briefly on several large oil paintings in their gilded frames. She felt sure that the paintings had not been selected by Polly Rutherford.

Taylor had seemed perfectly at home in his casual beach house, and Leah was interested to see that he seemed equally at home among the priceless antiques and old-world grandeur of his city dwelling.

Mrs. Cambridge settled herself in a large wing-back chair, and acting the hostess in what had once been her home, she indicated that Leah should sit on the sofa. Taylor stood by his mother as the three chatted. Finally, Mrs. Cambridge's fingers closed over a tiny box that rested on the occasional table next to her chair. She handed it quietly to her son.

"Thank you, mother."

"You don't know how pleased I am to give it back to you," she said. She started to rise. "I'll leave you alone now while you give Leah the ring."

"Oh, no, please stay," Taylor encouraged her. "We've already had our private moment when I proposed in the taxi. When I made the *official* proposal," he said, with a wink at Leah.

"Well, I would love to see Leah's reaction."

"Yes, don't leave now," Leah added her plea.

Mrs. Cambridge sat back down in her chair.

Taylor crossed over to where Leah sat and bent his head close to hers as he opened the ring box. Leah exclaimed over its unusual beauty as it came into sight. It was a fairly wide gold band with two smaller threads of gold that encircled it and then formed a more complicated pattern that held a beautiful large marquise diamond. Next to it in the box was a simple gold band, the wedding band.

Taylor withdrew the engagement ring from the box and slipped it onto Leah's finger. She stretched her hand out, holding it up to the light to admire the ring.

"Thank you. I love it."

"My grandfather had it made for my grandmother —ninety years ago," said Mrs. Cambridge. "Both rings were worn so thin at the bottom that we had to have them repaired."

Taylor put the box containing the wedding band into his pocket. "I'll hang on to this," he said. Then he seated himself beside Leah, and the three talked a bit more.

It was decided that Leah would stay at Taylor's house for a few days, and Taylor invited his mother to stay, too, so that she and his prospective bride could become better acquainted. After that, Leah and Taylor would fly down to Charlotte so that Taylor could meet her parents, and they would announce their engagement. Taylor would not be able to stay long—he would fly back to take care of his business while Leah remained in Charlotte to prepare for the wedding.

It was happening so fast. *Is it happening too fast?* Leah questioned herself. Not that she had any doubts about her love for Taylor. She stole a glance at him as he spoke with his mother, and watched his relaxed demeanor. He was totally confident. She knew he felt that once a thing had been decided, there was no need to act as if there were anything further to discuss. Leah's relationship with Taylor had been impetuous from the very beginning. That was the way Taylor was, and that was the way he made her feel.

She felt his strong hand close over hers, and a warm feeling spread through her. As they conversed, she noticed that Mrs. Cambridge was looking fondly at both of them. She felt some measure of relief at the realization that Taylor's mother seemed to regard her as something very good in her son's life. She wondered if the mother had worried much about her son in former years.

Taylor went out late that afternoon. He said he had something important to attend to and would not be gone long.

"Nothing serious, I hope?" his mother asked.

Taylor just shook his head.

"Is he always this secretive about his work?" Leah asked Mrs. Cambridge lightly after Taylor had gone.

"He probably just feels we wouldn't be interested."

Leah enjoyed the time she spent with Taylor's mother, and by that evening, Mrs. Cambridge had convinced her to call her Julia. Taylor returned after a few hours, and they had a very fine dinner prepared by Taylor's cook.

The next morning, Taylor said again that he must go out for a little while. Leah tried not to eavesdrop, but she couldn't help but notice Julia pull her son aside and speak to him quietly. It seems she was reminding him that it was Saturday and asking him if it was really necessary for him to go in to work on that particular

Saturday. Leah realized that Taylor's mother was already concerned about his treatment of his new fiancée.

Leah turned to speak to Julia after Taylor left. "Don't worry about me," she said. "I have some shopping I'd like to do, and nothing would suit me better than to get it done this morning."

Julia offered to accompany her, but Leah said she knew exactly what she wanted to buy and that it would be a quick, unexciting trip. She let Julia telephone for a taxi for her.

When Leah returned from her shopping, she was surprised to hear Julia say that Taylor was already back home.

"He's in the library," said his mother, "and he has someone with him—Polly Rutherford."

Leah was vexed with herself at her own reaction to this news. There was a tightening in her stomach and a cold feeling in her heart. She supposed every woman felt that way when she knew her man was with a woman with whom he had once been intimate. But she knew that it had happened a long time before and that she was being ridiculous. If she was going to marry Taylor, she would just have to accept the fact that he was going to be spending time with Polly. Polly was a long-time employee, after all. The thought occurred to her that Taylor and Polly might be discussing their attempts to help her in her career. She wondered if they would ask her to join them if they knew she was in the house.

"Would you like to see the clothes I bought?" Leah asked Taylor's mother, succeeding in her attempt to be cheerful. "I also bought a book to read."

"Oh, do you love to read as much as I do? I have a new book myself that I'm anxious to read. Maybe we can start our books after I look at your new clothes."

Leah showed Julia the new skirts and blouses that she had bought; then the two women went into the living room to begin their books. They had just gotten settled when Julia realized, with an exclamation, that she had left her reading glasses somewhere.

"I can't do without them," she said. "I remember where I left them—in the library."

"Let me get them for you," offered Leah, jumping to her feet. She started out of the room, then hesitated when she remembered that Taylor and Polly were in the library. "I wonder if I'll disturb them," she said.

"Oh, honey, I don't think so," said Julia, looking surprised. "But if you feel uncomfortable about it, I'll go get the glasses."

"No, no," protested Leah, "let me do it."

"Thank you," said Julia, but she gave Leah a sharp look, as if she wondered at Leah's unease.

Leah made her way to the back of the house where the library was located. As she approached the closed door of the library, she heard voices coming from within, voices that were raised a bit more than was necessary for normal conversation.

She hoped Taylor wouldn't think she was checking up on him—she wondered if she should knock. Instead, she quietly opened the door and took a step into the room. She stopped abruptly at the sight that met her eyes. Taylor and Polly were seated facing each other, heads close together, at a small table across the room. Taylor's fists were clenched, and when he looked up at Leah's entrance, she saw that his face was twisted with anger. Polly did not look up, but the room seemed so filled with tension and almost-tangible hostility that Leah was repelled. She started back involuntarily, saying, "I'm sorry," and began to close the door.

Polly still did not look up—her eyes were trained on Taylor—but she said in a flat voice, "Let her come in. She's going to hear it sooner or later."

Taylor got to his feet, walked over to Leah, and taking her hand, drew her into the room. Once inside the library, she remained standing, and Taylor stood to one side, folding his arms across his chest.

"Is something happening that I should know about?" Leah asked.

Taylor spoke to Polly. "Do you want to tell her, or should I?"

"Why don't you begin?" said Polly, the polite words spoken in a voice filled with rancor.

Taylor sighed. "You know, Leah, some days ago, Polly took your paintings and showed them to George Mayer. The day after she showed them to him, she came to give me a report. That was the day—the day of the night that you called me from Vero Beach. Remember?" The look he gave her was a kindly one, and Leah nodded, remembering the joyfulness of the phone call and remembering, also, Taylor's silence about Mayer's reaction to her work. "Polly seemed quite crestfallen," he said with a rueful smile. "She said that not only did the great man turn down a chance to exhibit your paintings but that he made some very derogatory—some very *nasty* comments about them and about the artist. The more I thought about it, the angrier I got."

"I wish you wouldn't," said Leah quickly. "It doesn't bother me."

"Hear him out, Leah," came Polly's abrupt voice.

Taylor flashed Polly a look of annoyance. "Finally, yesterday morning, I got angry enough to storm into his gallery."

"You didn't!"

"Yes, I did. But he wasn't there; they said he

wouldn't be back till late afternoon. So I waited till after I brought you here from the airport. Then I went back to the gallery. I gave Mayer a chance to speak for himself, and I'm glad I did. I told him he had every right to refuse to show your work but that his comments were way out of line."

Leah felt some confusion. She understood why Taylor would be angry with the art dealer, but that didn't completely explain the emotional tenor of the scene that was then taking place. There seemed to be conflict between Taylor and Polly as well as between Taylor and George Mayer, and when Polly at last turned her face to look at Leah, Leah was shocked at the hatred she saw in Polly's eyes.

"What comments did he make?" asked Leah, eyes round.

Polly pressed her lips together at Leah's question, but Taylor said, "They don't bear repeating. But when I repeated some of them to *him,* he denied ever making them! He said he had carefully listed his reasons for turning down the paintings in the letter he had given Polly. He was very surprised when I told him that Polly had given me no letter. He suggested I talk to Polly about it." He paused. "I couldn't track her down at the store this morning, so I left a message suggesting—"

"Demanding," threw in Polly.

"—that she meet me here as soon as she could. I also . . . suggested . . . that she bring the letter with her, and she was smart enough to do that."

Polly rose to her feet. Leah noticed that despite her hostility she was as perfectly groomed as ever—hair and makeup in place, clothes unrumpled. "So I came," she said. She looked around the room. "The last time I was in this room was many years ago. I was much younger—Taylor was much younger. This is the room we used when someone else was in the house. There's a lock on the door, you see. When no one else was at home, we went somewhere else—"

"Keep quiet!" Taylor burst out angrily. "You're speaking to my future wife. I think you've tried to hurt her enough. Besides, she's already forgiven my past . . . indiscretions." The look he gave Leah held a trace of uncertainty, and she gave him a smile that she hoped communicated reassurance.

Polly looked pointedly at the ring on Leah's finger. "She got what *she* wanted," she said. "After all these years of conniving females, one finally trapped you."

"That's enough, Polly," he said. "It astounds me that you would have the nerve to call someone else conniving. You're only making things worse by this line of talk."

Polly sat down again at the little table, defeated. "You may as well show her the letter. . . ."

For the first time, Leah noticed the piece of paper on the table. Taylor walked over, picked it up and handed it to her. He asked her to read it.

" 'My dear Mr. Cambridge,' " she read aloud, " 'I have always been greatly impressed with your protégés. Therefore, it surprises me that you would take under your wing one who is so obviously lacking in talent. . . .' " Leah stopped. "I'm too embarrassed to read this," she said.

"No, go on," Taylor urged her.

" 'Even primitive art requires a degree of skill, an eye for color and composition. While Miss DuChaine's best efforts are the skating scene and the summer boating scene . . .' " Leah looked up, dumfounded. "These don't sound like my paintings."

"They're not!" said Taylor with disgust, and he took the letter from her grasp.

Leah stared at Polly. "You mean you were passing off another artist's work as mine?" she asked.

Polly didn't answer, but Taylor nodded his head. "Her little scheme was destined to fail, of course," he said. "She couldn't have gone on deceiving us forever; not that it would have done her any good if she'd been able to. But the whole thing could have gone on a lot longer if she hadn't been so vindictive—if she hadn't gotten carried away with herself." He looked at Polly. "You took pleasure, didn't you, in making up those ugly remarks which you attributed to George Mayer. You just didn't count on touching off my anger the way you did. You didn't count on my going directly to the source." He shook his head. "Do you know how this disappoints me? I thought a great deal of our friendship . . . and our business relationship—"

"And I suppose I should be grateful for that!" Polly's voice shook with anger. "Grateful for a few kind words and a pat on the back . . . when we used to have so much more!"

"Polly, I'm deeply sorry that you were more involved in our relationship than I was. I deeply regret . . . it all. . . ."

Polly stood up, looking as if she had been slapped. "You just remember what I told you," she said to Leah, regarding her coldly. "I warned you . . . Just wait and see. . . ."

She started out of the room, but Taylor stopped her. "What is this all about!" he demanded.

Polly said nothing, so Taylor looked to Leah. "When did she speak with you?"

"She came to the hotel room once when you were away. I didn't think it important enough to bother you about. She said she wanted to warn me against you. . . ."

Taylor shook his head. "So you'd like to destroy my chance at happiness along with your own?" he asked Polly.

Polly moved toward the door. "Well, now it's your chance to destroy me," she said. "That should make you feel better. Why don't you fire me right now?"

"Polly, you know we can't work together . . . after all this. But I will help you. I'm sure I could help you get a job at one of the good galleries in Soho."

"Fine!" Polly said with contempt, and she walked out.

Taylor went quickly to Leah and put his arms around her. "I'm so sorry," he said. "We've learned a lot this morning, haven't we?"

"I can only feel sorry for her," said Leah. "She's so unhappy . . ."

"And can you forgive me—for my part in her unhappiness?"

"Yes. You didn't deliberately try to hurt her."

"It turns out you were right on target about Polly Rutherford. I apologize for not giving more weight to your intuition. She wanted to hurt you. Not because she didn't like you personally but because—"

"She was jealous!" finished Leah.

Taylor shook his head slowly. "I know the very paintings she brought to the dealers. They were done by the daughter of a friend of my father. My father took pity on her and bought them—they've been in the back storage bins at the store gallery for years. The only thing that surprises me is that the dealers took them as seriously as they did. They look like"— Taylor laughed as he searched for an appropriate comparison—"something *I* would paint! Polly took some acrylic paints and covered up the signatures, then added your signature."

"That poor artist," said Leah with feeling. "How awful to have your work regarded as a joke."

"I wouldn't worry about it," said Taylor, rubbing her arm. "I'm sure she's gone on to other things by now and wouldn't care what professional dealers think of her artistic attempts." He sat on the love seat behind them and drew Leah down beside him. He looked at her anxiously. "Did anything Polly say alter your feelings for me?"

"Of course not," said Leah lovingly.

"When she came to see you at the hotel, I'm sure she maligned my character—" Taylor began, but Leah stopped him.

"I think I know as much about your character as anyone," she assured him. "And the more I see, the more I like. I certainly wouldn't want people to judge *me* by my past mistakes."

Taylor was silent a moment. Then he said, "Now my only problem is to find another art buyer. It's a great job; it involves travel, meeting interesting people, seeing all kinds of fine art . . ."

Leah looked up to find his eyes fixed steadily on her.

"Oh, no!" she protested. "It's wonderful that you think a woman ought to be able to have a career of her own, but don't you think it's going a bit far to choose her career for her? Didn't you once mention that you were attracted by my 'creative solitude' and 'singleness of purpose'?"

"You're right, I wasn't really serious," he said, smiling. "The next thing I want to do is to pay another visit to George Mayer—this time with the authentic works of Leah DuChaine."

Leah thought back over the unpleasant scene that had just taken place in the room. Something Polly had said—or was it something in the letter?—was bothering her slightly. She turned to Taylor and took a breath.

"So, have you had many 'protégés'?" she asked him innocently.

Taylor laughed and took Leah by the shoulders. "I warn you; I'll shake you till your teeth rattle if you don't stop those thoughts from going through your head!"

"How do you know what my thoughts are?"

"I think I know very well. You're not *really* concerned about my past misdeeds as long as they remain in the past." He looked at her closely. "I think it's just that old objection you have to being just another girl in my harem."

"I suppose so," she admitted.

"Now listen to me," he said sternly. "I hate to spoil your illusions about my hopelessly scandalous past. Yes, I have given a helping hand to the careers of four artists—my protégés, if you will. But I have had a close romantic relationship with only *one* of those talented artists."

"Oh." Leah tried to act as if it didn't matter.

"I can see I *will* have to shake you!" he threatened. "That *one* artist is you!"

"Oh," she repeated, her lips curving upward.

"Now, are you going to apologize for your thoughts?"

"Taylor, I've never heard of anything so outrageous. Apologizing for one's thoughts, indeed!" But she turned and put her arms around him and kissed him tenderly. His arms went around her and pulled her close as he returned her kiss with a fiery one of his own.

Suddenly, Leah pulled away, and her hand flew to her face. "Your mother's glasses!" she said with consternation. "I nearly forgot!" She leaped up and ran to pick up the pair of spectacles that she saw resting on a nearby table. "That's what I came in here for, to get her glasses," she explained, and she went hastily out the library door.

Two days later, Taylor left the house early in the morning. He returned late in the afternoon and found his mother and Leah waiting for him. He had a satisfied look on his face.

"George Mayer's not a bad fellow," he said.

"Well, tell us, son," said his mother with a touch of impatience. "What did he say?"

"He jumped at the chance to represent you," he said to Leah, and she flung her arms around his neck.

"Oh, if he had anything nice to say about my work, please tell me! My ego's taken a real beating lately."

"He had lots of admiring things to say," said Taylor, his voice muffled by Leah's hair. "Things such as . . . beautiful . . . innovative . . . exciting . . ." He whispered in her ear. "He was speaking of your paintings, but those words describe you."

"We must celebrate!" decided Julia. "Come into the drawing room. There's sherry—and there's some champagne in the refrigerator!"

"And then we'll have dinner out. Your choice," Taylor told Leah.

Leah followed them into the drawing room. She felt bedazzled by her good fortune. The following morning, she and Taylor planned to fly to Charlotte. The wedding plans would be made; the ceremony would be held. Then would begin the adventure of her life with Taylor.

Chapter Twelve

As Leah traveled down U.S. Route 1, she thought about the solitary journey she had taken a month and a half earlier down the very same route. At that time, she had felt complete in herself. All her dreams had seemed to have their source in her own mind and heart then. She had known exactly where her life was headed, had not foreseen the startling changes that six weeks would bring.

This time, she was not driving the car; she was a passenger. She wore a lightweight bright burgundy traveling suit with a white embroidered blouse. Her hair was arranged in an intricate woven style, curving about her head. When she shook it, a few grains of rice flew out of the strands.

"Are you tired?" One of Taylor's hands closed over hers as he drove with the other one, and he smiled at her with the smile that she knew would always make her heart flutter a little bit. "We'll be there in about an hour."

"I'm just fine. Don't forget, I've driven this route all by myself, and I didn't have the slightest bit of trouble."

She studied Taylor as he gave his attention to the road, her eyes resting contemplatively on his rugged profile and strong jaw. She felt a quiet pride at the thought of how handsome he had looked in his wedding suit earlier that day. All the women present at the ceremony had not been able to keep their eyes off him. After an hour at the reception at her parents' house, Leah had left her simple white gown and gossamer veil in an elegant heap on her mother's bed, to be attended to by someone else while she hurriedly changed her clothes. Then she and Taylor had run with ducked heads through her parents' front door, through the lines of friends and relatives and a storm of rice till they were safe in his waiting car.

"The whole thing went pretty well, don't you think?" Leah asked him. "Was it as trying as you thought it would be?"

"I never said I thought it would be a trial."

"You didn't have to," she said, smiling.

"I think it went very well," he reassured her. "Your mother is a woman with very good taste."

"Do you mean because she had the good sense to keep it a small wedding?" she asked him, amused. "I used to be under the impression that you took to large formal affairs the way a duck takes to water."

"Yes, but you know me better than that by now. I'll tell you what the finest moment of the whole occasion was."

"When we got into the car after it was over?" she guessed.

"No, it wasn't when we got into the car or even when we turned out of the driveway. It was when we turned the corner out of sight of everybody and found ourselves alone—just starting our journey."

"Yes, that was the best," she agreed softly, thinking back to the moment he described. Just after turning the corner, they had looked at each other with excited eyes, and the very air in the moving car had seemed to take on a special aura of love and magic. It was a cool, still September day, perfect weather for heading south. "And now we'll have a night in 'my' room at the Ocean Inn; then three weeks in the Caribbean. Who could ask for a better honeymoon?"

The Caribbean honeymoon had been a gift from Taylor's father, but it had been Taylor's idea to spend their wedding night where he and Leah had met, at the Ocean Inn. Joyce Becker had arranged it so they would have the very same room in which Leah had stayed.

There was time now for Leah to think, and she thought about her future and how she was going to handle it. She was able to consider it now without the clutch of apprehension that she felt when she had first begun to realize that Taylor was becoming a part of her life. She was confident now of her ability to hold tightly to her dreams in spite of the distractions with which her new life would tempt her. And yet . . . sometimes she still liked to have a little reassurance.

She turned to her husband. "Taylor."

"Mm-hm?"

"Do you still think I can do it? Do you think I can work at being a good artist . . . and still have time to make you happy?" It was a discussion they had had before, and she wondered if Taylor would grow annoyed that she had brought it up again. She looked at him curiously and saw that she had nothing to fear.

"You're a very special person, Leah. You have talent and determination. You can have anything, be anything you want. Just sharing your life is enough to make me happy."

At last, they found themselves just a few miles from Vero Beach. A sudden memory hit Leah, and she chuckled.

"Something amusing?" he inquired.

"Oh, no. At least . . . I can't tell you."

He laughed. "Now you have to tell me, you know."

She realized she was caught. "I know. Well . . ." she began hesitantly, "you might look upon this as a kind of confession."

"I'm listening," he said, suddenly alert.

"Did you know that I didn't really *want* to like you when I first met you?"

Taylor laughed again. "That's it? You made no secret of *that* fact!"

"No, that's not all. I didn't want to fall for you, but it was hard to get you out of my mind."

"It was?"

"Yes. I was told that if I wanted to forget you I should either just stop thinking about you, *or* . . . I should spend a lot of time with you, get to know you so well that I would discover you weren't so wonderful, after all. I'm sure you're aware of the connection between familiarity and contempt. So I had an ulterior motive when I agreed to go to New York with you that first time. I was hoping that my . . . attraction . . . to you would lessen."

A frown appeared between Taylor's eyes. "And what was the result of this little experiment in familiarity?"

Her voice grew very quiet. "It wasn't contempt."

"What was the result?" he persisted.

"Taylor, you know I love you to distraction. If we weren't in a moving vehicle, I'd prove it right now."

She felt the car surge forward slightly and noticed that his foot was exerting a little more pressure on the accelerator.

"Who was it," asked Taylor, "that gave you such excellent advice—to spend more time with me?"

"My friend Rhoda Hughes."

"Bless her." He grinned.

When they pulled into the parking lot of the Ocean Inn, they noticed that there was more activity than when Leah had arrived in August, but it was quiet enough for their taste. They checked in, then headed toward their room, Taylor with a suitcase in each hand. Leah carried her purse and the bottle of champagne that she had not been surprised to find in the trunk of the car.

"I feel almost as if I'm coming home," she commented. She stood on the deck facing the sea as Taylor fit the key into the lock. He opened the door and shoved the suitcases inside. Leah made a move to enter the room, but before she could, Taylor gathered her up with one sweeping motion and stepped into the room with her in his arms.

"Oh, yes, I almost forgot," she murmured.

He stood holding her for a moment, looked searchingly at her. Her skin was glowing, her eyes a shining deep blue. "Why *did* you dislike me so much when you first met me?" he demanded. "I found *you* very appealing."

"I found you appealing, too," she said with downcast eyes. "I just hadn't expected you to disrupt my life the way you did." She looked at him accusingly.

"And you did try to seduce me, you know. Almost the first moment we met. My first impression of you was *not* one of a gentleman."

He sighed as he placed her gently on the floor. "I suppose I'm going to hear about that for the rest of my life."

"Of course you are."

"Actually, I don't mind in the least. Looking back, much of that memory is very pleasant."

Leah set the bottle of champagne on the dresser, then removed her light jacket and draped it over the back of a chair. She turned back to Taylor. "We've got the champagne," she pointed out. "Isn't it time we take it out on the deck and enjoy the evening breezes as we sip it?" She expected, somehow, that Taylor planned to re-enact their first meeting—only this time, of course, the evening would end quite differently.

But Taylor closed the door softly, turned the lock and said in a firm voice, "Not on your life."

He laced his fingers through hers and drew her toward the bed, where he sat and pulled her down beside him. He looked at the top of her head. "Isn't there a single strategic pin that I can pull out of your hair and the whole thing will come down?" he asked.

"No, but—" She quickly withdrew a dozen hairpins one after the other, let them drop to the floor, and her hair tumbled loose.

Taylor buried his face in the fragrant blonde tangles. His arms went around her body in a powerful embrace, and she relaxed against him, molding her soft curves to him. He covered her mouth with a hungry kiss.

"Taylor."

He pulled back reluctantly and looked at her with slumberous eyes.

"Taylor, was it difficult for you?" she demanded breathlessly. "When I was staying with you in the hotel? You told me once that you didn't trust yourself to be alone in the same room with me. But then you seemed to have no problem at all in the hotel suite—"

Taylor groaned. "Oh, baby, you don't understand yet? To see you all warm and sleepy in the morning, to hear the shower running, knowing the water was caressing what I wanted to caress—" He stroked the tender curves of her body as he spoke. "And that backrub I gave you. That was foolhardy; do you know that? It was almost my undoing. If the knock on the door hadn't come at that precise moment—"

"Then how—"

"How was I able to remain such a gentleman?" He smiled. "It's very simple. It's just that you—Leah DuChaine—taught me that there are some things more important than physical gratification." He pressed her gently backward. "But frankly, at this moment"—his voice deepened and his caresses grew more intimate—"I can't for the life of me think of what those other things could be . . ."

"Taylor . . ."

But his lips found hers, and he silenced her with a deep, passionate kiss. Tenderly, he gathered her to himself, and Leah surrendered herself to a love that made the rest of her life till now seem only a prelude.

IT'S YOUR OWN SPECIAL TIME

Contemporary romances for today's women.
Each month, six very special love stories will be yours
from SILHOUETTE.

$1.75 each

☐ 100 Stanford	☐ 127 Roberts	☐ 155 Hampson	☐ 182 Clay
☐ 101 Hardy	☐ 128 Hampson	☐ 156 Sawyer	☐ 183 Stanley
☐ 102 Hastings	☐ 129 Converse	☐ 157 Vitek	☐ 184 Hardy
☐ 103 Cork	☐ 130 Hardy	☐ 158 Reynolds	☐ 185 Hampson
☐ 104 Vitek	☐ 131 Stanford	☐ 159 Tracy	☐ 186 Howard
☐ 105 Eden	☐ 132 Wisdom	☐ 160 Hampson	☐ 187 Scott
☐ 106 Dailey	☐ 133 Rowe	☐ 161 Trent	☐ 188 Cork
☐ 107 Bright	☐ 134 Charles	☐ 162 Ashby	☐ 189 Stephens
☐ 108 Hampson	☐ 135 Logan	☐ 163 Roberts	☐ 190 Hampson
☐ 109 Vernon	☐ 136 Hampson	☐ 164 Browning	☐ 191 Browning
☐ 110 Trent	☐ 137 Hunter	☐ 165 Young	☐ 192 John
☐ 111 South	☐ 138 Wilson	☐ 166 Wisdom	☐ 193 Trent
☐ 112 Stanford	☐ 139 Vitek	☐ 167 Hunter	☐ 194 Barry
☐ 113 Browning	☐ 140 Erskine	☐ 168 Carr	☐ 195 Dailey
☐ 114 Michaels	☐ 142 Browning	☐ 169 Scott	☐ 196 Hampson
☐ 115 John	☐ 143 Roberts	☐ 170 Ripy	☐ 197 Summers
☐ 116 Lindley	☐ 144 Goforth	☐ 171 Hill	☐ 198 Hunter
☐ 117 Scott	☐ 145 Hope	☐ 172 Browning	☐ 199 Roberts
☐ 118 Dailey	☐ 146 Michaels	☐ 173 Camp	☐ 200 Lloyd
☐ 119 Hampson	☐ 147 Hampson	☐ 174 Sinclair	☐ 201 Starr
☐ 120 Carroll	☐ 148 Cork	☐ 175 Jarrett	☐ 202 Hampson
☐ 121 Langan	☐ 149 Saunders	☐ 176 Vitek	☐ 203 Browning
☐ 122 Scofield	☐ 150 Major	☐ 177 Dailey	☐ 204 Carroll
☐ 123 Sinclair	☐ 151 Hampson	☐ 178 Hampson	☐ 205 Maxam
☐ 124 Beckman	☐ 152 Halston	☐ 179 Beckman	☐ 206 Manning
☐ 125 Bright	☐ 153 Dailey	☐ 180 Roberts	☐ 207 Windham
☐ 126 St. George	☐ 154 Beckman	☐ 181 Terrill	

IT'S YOUR OWN SPECIAL TIME

Contemporary romances for today's women.
Each month, six very special love stories will be yours
from SILHOUETTE. Look for them wherever books are sold
or order now from the coupon below.

$1.95 each

☐ 208 Halston	☐ 225 St. George	☐ 242 Brooke	☐ 259 English
☐ 209 LaDame	☐ 226 Hamson	☐ 243 Saunders	☐ 260 Martin
☐ 210 Eden	☐ 227 Beckman	☐ 244 Sinclair	☐ 261 Saunders
☐ 211 Walters	☐ 228 King	☐ 245 Trent	☐ 262 John
☐ 212 Young	☐ 229 Thornton	☐ 246 Carroll	☐ 263 Wilson
☐ 213 Dailey	☐ 230 Stevens	☐ 247 Halldorson	☐ 264 Vine
☐ 214 Hampson	☐ 231 Dailey	☐ 248 St. George	☐ 265 Adams
☐ 215 Roberts	☐ 232 Hampson	☐ 249 Scofield	☐ 266 Trent
☐ 216 Saunders	☐ 233 Vernon	☐ 250 Hampson	☐ 267 Chase
☐ 217 Vitek	☐ 234 Smith	☐ 251 Wilson	☐ 268 Hunter
☐ 218 Hunter	☐ 235 James	☐ 252 Roberts	☐ 269 Smith
☐ 219 Cork	☐ 236 Maxam	☐ 253 James	☐ 270 Camp
☐ 220 Hampson	☐ 237 Wilson	☐ 254 Palmer	☐ 271 Allison
☐ 221 Browning	☐ 238 Cork	☐ 255 Smith	☐ 272 Forrest
☐ 222 Carroll	☐ 239 McKay	☐ 256 Hampson	☐ 273 Beckman
☐ 223 Summers	☐ 240 Hunter	☐ 257 Hunter	
☐ 224 Langan	☐ 241 Wisdom	☐ 258 Ashby	

SILHOUETTE BOOKS, Department SB/1

1230 Avenue of the Americas
New York, NY 10020

Please send me the books I have checked above. I am enclosing $_____
(please add 75¢ to cover postage and handling. NYS and NYC residents please
add appropriate sales tax). Send check or money order—no cash or C.O.D.'s
please. Allow six weeks for delivery.

NAME _____

ADDRESS _____

CITY _____ STATE/ZIP _____